Countdown to Mardi Gras!

Dianna Houx

Contents

Reading Order

Holiday Countdown Books:
1.) Countdown to Christmas
2.) Countdown to Valentine's Day
3.) Countdown to Easter
4.) Countdown to Mother's Day
5.) Countdown to 4th of July!
6.) Countdown to Halloween!
7.) Countdown to Thanksgiving!
8.) Countdown to Christmas Eve!
9.) Countdown to New Beginnings
10.) Countdown to a Wedding
11.) Countdown to Mardi Gras!

I recommend reading the books in order. There is an overarching storyline that starts in book 1 and continues throughout the series. Plus, it's more fun that way!

Days till Mardi Gras

-Twenty-

Grace stepped onto the front porch, her hand instinctively reaching for the doorknob. As she twisted the knob, she paused, an unfamiliar feeling rising up from the pit of her stomach: detachment. She shook her head, confused as to where the feeling had come from. She'd lived here for over twenty years—was two weeks away all it took for this place to no longer feel like home? Really?

"This is crazy," she muttered, turning the knob with more force than necessary. The door flew open, Grace *just* managing to catch it before it banged into the wall. As the familiar scents of coffee, pastries, and something unmistakably 'home' wafted over her, she began to feel more at ease. That is, until she walked into the dining room.

"I'm back!" she exclaimed as she entered the room.

The friendly chatter ceased as six sets of eyes turned to stare at her.

"Um, hi," Grace said, waving awkwardly at Granny, Gladys, Emilio, Rebekah, Grant, and Molly.

Granny was the first to speak. "Welcome home, sweetheart," she said as she rose from her seat and approached Grace for a hug. "We've missed you."

"I missed you, too!" Grace replied, returning Granny's hug.

She turned to hug Gladys next, then made her way through the rest of the group before ending with Molly.

"We're happy you're back," Molly stated warmly.

There was a subtle shift in the atmosphere. As Grace looked at the others, she discovered they were watching silently. "You guys are really creeping me out," Grace joked. "What's going on?"

Molly gave her a reassuring pat on the back. "It's just... you were supposed to be back a week ago, and we're running out of time if we plan to pull off another Anti-Valentine's Day Experience."

Why did she suddenly feel like an employee who had inconvenienced her boss instead of a member of the family? She tried to shrug it off, certain she was reading more into it than there was. After all, she had extended her time away longer than anyone had expected—including her. All of her fears of not getting along with Cole once they had unlimited time together had proved to be unfounded. Instead, the opposite had happened, and she hadn't been ready to leave when it was time. But can anyone really blame her? What woman wants to leave her husband to return to work, especially when that husband is Cole Reed!

Grace cleared her throat. "Um, about that," she began, unsure of how to break the news. "I don't want to do the 'Anti-Valentine's Day Experience' this year."

There—she'd said it. She chanced a glance at Rebekah and saw relief on her face. Apparently her friend was no more interested in reliving the events of last year than Grace was.

"I understand how you feel," Molly said through gritted teeth. "But do I need to remind you we still need to keep hosting events at the B&B? Getting married didn't change our financial situation." She paused and narrowed her eyes at Grace. "Unless you guys won the lottery while you were gone?"

"No, of course not," Grace replied with a laugh. "I'm not saying I won't host an event, I'm just saying I don't want the event to be for Valentine's Day."

Molly exchanged an unreadable glance with Grant before turning back to Grace. "Soooo, what then?"

The moment she'd been dreading was finally here. Her friends were either about to think she was a genius or a complete dunce. Either way, it was time to rip the proverbial Band-Aid off. "I was thinking we could do a Mardi Gras event!"

"Ooh, like in New Orleans?" Emilio asked.

Grace beamed at him. "Exactly!"

"I don't know," Rebekah interjected. "While I would love nothing more than to skip Valentine's Day this year, I've been to Mardi Gras in New Orleans, and I just can't see us pulling that off on such short notice. They plan their events a year in advance—you've given us, what, two weeks?"

"I agree with Rebekah," Molly said, clearly perplexed by the unexpected idea. "What would that even look like? That's the kind of event you need a big city for, and big city we ain't!"

Gladys nudged Granny with her elbow. "We think this sounds like a great idea, don't we, Josie?"

Granny frowned. "It could be fun," she said slowly. "But I think I need a little more convincing. I've never been to a Mardi Gras celebration, but I've heard they aren't exactly family-friendly..."

Luckily, Grace had expected their objections and had come prepared. "I think families go to these events all the time," she began, determined to overcome that objection first. "But even if they don't, that doesn't mean ours can't be family-friendly!" She smiled at Granny, then continued. "Here's what I'm thinking: we'll have a week-long carnival that starts on the Tuesday before Mardi Gras, with events each day. I'm talking 5Ks, Cajun cook-offs, scavenger hunts, parades, concerts—you name it!"

She paused to take a breath and gauge their reactions, but so far, nobody seemed swayed in either direction. "For the grand finale, we'll host a masquerade ball on Mardi Gras!"

Gladys clapped her hands together. "This sounds like so much fun!"

"Thank you, Gladys!" Grace beamed at the woman, thankful at least one person was on her side. "Me personally, I feel this is much more exciting than another boring Valentine's Day celebration."

Rebekah cleared her throat. "Again, I am in complete agreement on that point, but how do you plan to overcome the lack of time? What you just described will take a lot of work. In fact, I'm pretty sure this would be our biggest event to date."

Grace snorted. "Hasn't that been our M.O. for every event we've done thus far?" She looked around at their faces, each one showing some level of doubt—except for Gladys, bless that woman. "Come on, guys," Grace chided. "So far, we've put on three last-minute weddings—including mine. Two last-minute Christmas Experiences, and an extremely last-minute anniversary party." She turned to Molly and gave her a look. "Not to mention the Mother's Day Experience YOU scheduled an entire week early and dropped on me with little more than a day's notice."

Molly winced at the reminder. "I see what you're saying, but a carnival? How on earth will we pull that off? You usually have to book those at least a year in advance."

"For the warmer months," Grace informed her. "Carnivals aren't booked up in the winter due to weather, and they're more than happy to accept bookings. I know this because I've already spoken to the owners of a few of them."

"What about the parade?" Rebekah asked, her pen tapping out a rapid staccato as she eyed the growing list of to-do items in her notebook. "Mardi Gras parade floats are pretty extravagant, I doubt they throw them together in a couple of weeks."

It was tempting to roll her eyes, but Grace managed to refrain. Why were they being so difficult? She should have asked Lyda to meet her here this morning. She was always up for a challenge, regardless of the size or practicality of the mission. "I have no doubt the townspeople will rally behind this event. With enough help, we should have zero problems getting everything done in time. In fact, if we make it a competition, I bet things will get done long before we need them to be!"

She paused again, willing everyone to see reason and agree to her plan. "So, who's with me?"

"You know I am!" Gladys said enthusiastically.

Granny nodded, though she still didn't seem entirely convinced.

Emilio and Grant exchanged looks. "This isn't going to be cheap," Emilio pointed out.

"But if you manage to pull it off, it could make a ton of money," Grant conceded.

That counted as two more 'yeses' as far as Grace was concerned. Which meant, four down, two to go. She turned to Rebekah and raised a brow.

Rebekah sighed, resignation clear on her face. "Fine. Send me a list of everything you want to do, and I'll get started on a plan."

Grace squealed. "Thank you!" She rushed over and hugged Rebekah from behind. "This is going to be so much fun!" she gushed.

"We'll see," Rebekah said skeptically.

All that was left was Molly. Grace turned to her, a pleading look on her face. "Please!" She tented her hands in front of her and gave Molly her best puppy dog look.

Molly rolled her eyes, a smile on her face. "This is significantly more work than I expected, but I can see the potential."

"Yay!" Grace threw her arms around Molly's neck.

"Don't thank me yet," Molly cautioned. "We still need to take this before the town council. If they approve, then we'll have to see if we get enough volunteers to pull this off."

Grace was so confident neither of those would be a problem, she waved off Molly's concerns. "It's going to be great, guys!"

Grant handed Eliza to Molly, then excused himself. "I'm not sure why a newly married woman wants to take on a project this big so soon after her honeymoon, but I'll do what I can to support you." He gave Grace a hug. "Welcome back," he said. "You have been missed, even if we didn't initially show it."

Emilio stood and gave Grace a small smile, then followed Grant out to their cars.

Molly left next, baby Eliza in tow. That left the four of them.

As soon as Grace took a seat, Rebekah stood and gathered her things. "I've got to run, but I want to hear all about your trip as soon as I get back," she told Grace.

Grace wanted to protest. She'd been looking forward to catching up with everyone, but she didn't want to appear selfish. "I'm looking forward to it," she said instead, making a concerted effort to hide her disappointment.

"I'm afraid we need to go, too," Granny said as she and Gladys pushed back their chairs. "We've got some errands to run before we meet Julian and Earl for lunch at Addie's." She paused to kiss the top of Grace's head. "I'm so glad you're back. We'll catch up later as well, okay?"

Unable to trust her voice, Grace smiled and nodded as she watched them leave. It's not like this was the first time people had places to be; in fact, it was normal. It's just she had really been looking forward to seeing everyone again. For the first time—in as long as she could remember—she was completely alone.

She looked around at the house she'd spent the majority of her life in. The last time she'd been here, she'd been a single woman; now, she was married. She, Grace Parker, was now Grace Reed. It was hard to fathom. Nothing was different, yet everything was different at the same time, and she had no idea how to handle it. With nothing else to do, she cleared the breakfast dishes, loaded the dishwasher, then grabbed her keys to go back home.

Startled, she looked down at the keys in her hand. When had this place stopped being home?

***

Once she arrived back at the farm, Grace saddled up her favorite horse, then rode off in search of Cole. She knew he was busy, but after the morning she'd had, she needed the comfort she knew he'd give.

It didn't take long to find him. All she had to do was follow the sound of the tractor. When she rode up beside him, he took one look at her, put the brake on, then hopped from the tractor to the back of the horse.

"What's wrong?" he asked, his arms circling her waist as he pulled her close.

She leaned her head back against his chest and closed her eyes. "Granny's home no longer feels like home," she said glumly. "Worse than that, they all left soon after I got there. I went from being needed to no one needing me at all."

Cole's arms tightened as he gently rocked her back and forth. "Isn't this a good thing?" he asked gently.

Grace tilted her face up to look at him. "What do you mean?"

He dropped a kiss on her upturned nose. "When we first met, you felt trapped, remember? You'd been Granny's caregiver for years, were on the verge of losing your home, and felt forced into a job you weren't sure you wanted."

There were no lies in that statement, though she did appreciate him leaving out the part about Hunter and Rebekah. "So you're saying I should be glad no one needs me anymore?"

Cole shook his head, then rested his cheek against hers. "First of all, that's not true," he replied. "*I* need you very much."

Touched by his words, she kissed his cheek as she threaded their fingers together. "I need you too," she whispered. "Though I'm sure you can see that," she said with a laugh.

He stared into her eyes for a moment, as if trying to find the right words to say. "Granny, Gladys, and the rest of the gang will always be family. I have no doubt that you are as important to them as they are to you," he said gently. "Having their own lives doesn't make those things less true."

Grace knew he was right but still couldn't come to terms with how quickly things had changed. "I guess I just don't understand," she admitted. "I spent a good portion of our honeymoon worried about Granny and how things were going at home without me. Now I find out that all my worrying was for nothing—which I know is a good thing," she hurried to add. "It's just, well, you know what I mean."

Cole nodded. "Transitions are hard," he said wisely. "I'm sure once you throw yourself into planning a new event, things will normalize. But for now, maybe you should consider writing. It might help to get all your feelings down."

Writing didn't seem like a terrible idea. It would give her something to do while she was in the in-between phase of waiting on the town council meeting.

"Thank you," she said, glad she'd come to see him, if not a little guilty for interrupting his work. She let go of one of his hands and reached up to pull his mouth down to hers. Regardless of all the changes in her life, one thing remained the same: she loved this man with all her heart.

Reluctantly, he climbed off the horse and back into the tractor. "Does this mean you'll be waiting for me when I'm finished later today?"

"How about I do you one better and bring you lunch?"

His lips turned up into a grin. "There's nothing I'd like more!" He tipped his hat, then got back to work, whistling a cheerful tune as he went.

Grace smiled as she watched him go. Maybe things weren't so bad after all.

-Nineteen-

Rebekah walked into the dining room and glanced over at Grace. "What are you doing?" she asked, her curiosity piqued.

"I'm writing a book," Grace replied, her gaze never leaving the notebook she was scribbling in.

She cocked her head. "Oh really? I had no idea you wanted to be a writer."

"Well, now you do!" Grace exclaimed with fake enthusiasm.

Still not quite buying her friend's newfound interest in writing, Rebekah crossed her arms and gave Grace a haughty look. "Okay, Miss Writer, what do you have so far?"

Grace gave her a sheepish look. She'd been sitting at the table for almost an hour and only had one sentence to show for it, but she just knew this sentence was a masterpiece and worth every second. She cleared her throat, then held her notebook in front of her as if she were reading from an ancient scroll.

"It was a dark and stormy night," she read in a spooky voice.

Seconds passed as Rebekah waited for Grace to continue. When she remained silent, Rebekah rolled her eyes. "Seriously?"

"It's a work in progress," Grace said defensively. "Sheesh, everyone's a critic these days."

Rebekah snorted. "That is the most clichéd, insipid thing you could possibly write!"

"Oh yeah?" Grace snarked, hurt by her friend's cruel words. "Do you think you could do better?"

She went silent for a moment, her eyes glazing over as she considered her words. "The sun had long since set, darkness shrouding every corner in black. Wind howled through the trees, the branches tapping against the windowpane as raindrops rapped an accompanying rhythm."

Grace's mouth gaped open as she stared in shock. When she recovered, she ripped out her page and began to write out Rebekah's sentences. "I'm stealing that," she announced.

"How about you tell me why you're really doing this?" Rebekah prodded. "We both know you don't really want to be a writer."

Even though Rebekah was right, her words stung a little. What if this *had* been a dream of hers? Would she still be so quick to judge this harshly? Or was Grace being overly sensitive? It was likely the latter, but that only helped her feel a little better.

"Um, well, I've had a hard time adjusting to things," Grace admitted. "For some reason, life feels so different now, even though the only thing that changed was my last name, address, and relationship status!" She attempted to keep her tone light, but could tell by the softening of the look on Rebekah's face that she'd failed. "Anyway, Cole suggested I write so..."

"I'm pretty sure he meant you should journal," Rebekah said gently. "Not write a novel."

Hmm, that made more sense. Why she thought he meant otherwise was anyone's guess. Somewhat relieved, she closed her notebook and pushed it away. "What's new with you?" she asked, anxious to change the subject.

Rebekah pulled out a chair and took a seat opposite Grace. "Oh, you know, the usual." She scrunched her nose. "A kid's birthday party, a baby shower, a funeral..."

Grace's eyes widened. "You planned a party for a funeral?"

She nodded. "Worse than that, I planned it with the person it's for."

"I'm sorry, what?" Grace asked, unable to process that bit of information. "Did you use an ouija board?" She winced. "Sorry, that was insensitive."

"No worries," Rebekah said, waving her off. "It's actually a sad but inspiring story..."

"You should see the party she has planned for after the funeral. There isn't a hint of black in sight! But enough about me, tell me all about your honeymoon." She blushed. "Well, maybe not *all* about it!"

How much should she share? "Well..."

"Well what?" Rebekah asked, her forehead creasing.

Grace took a deep breath. "We didn't actually go," she reluctantly admitted.

"Please don't tell me Cole backed out on your honeymoon so he could work," Rebekah pleaded. "Because if you do, I'm going to kill him."

"No, of course not!" Grace said, anxious to defend Cole.

Rebekah narrowed her eyes. "Then what happened?"

This was so embarrassing, Grace willed her phone to ring so she'd have an excuse to put an end to this humiliating conversation. When that didn't happen, she sucked in another breath; they really should have come up with a story before they decided to come back from their honeymoon. "So, it's like this," Grace began. "You know how we went back to the farm after the wedding, right?"

When Rebekah nodded, Grace continued. "We were supposed to drive to Hot Springs the next morning, but... I didn't want to."

"What do you mean you didn't want to?" Rebekah asked, an incredulous look on her face.

"I mean, I didn't want to spend six hours in a car," Grace explained, her cheeks reddening in embarrassment. "Up till that point, I'd spent so little time with Cole, it was nice to just be together, you know?"

Rebekah nodded, a grin spreading across her face. "I think I'm picking up what you're putting down."

She waggled her eyebrow, which only made Grace blush harder.

"Anyway, I knew we needed to go somewhere, or the temptation to work might get the better of Cole. But since I still didn't want to spend that much time in the car, we agreed to go to Branson instead."

When Rebekah remained silent, Grace continued. "It's the off-season, so I was able to book a condo at a resort for like, a third of the normal price! We spent our days hiking, touring museums, or curled up in front of the fireplace. That probably sounds pretty boring, but to me, it was magical!"

"That sounds like you guys," Rebekah said slowly. "In a good way," she hurried to add.

Now that she was spilling her guts, she felt the need to continue. "We actually got back about a week ago," she admitted guiltily.

The look on Rebekah's face was unreadable, her silence causing Grace anxiety.

"I needed time to adjust to my new life," Grace said, her tone becoming defensive. "I've spent most of my life in this house, and while I've stayed with Cole at the farm before, actually living there is a whole new ballgame." She shook her head, the struggle to communicate her feelings difficult to overcome. "I just—"

Rebekah reached across the table and took Grace's hand. "It's okay," she said, her tone soothing. "If you remember, it wasn't that long ago I was in that same boat when I moved here. If anyone understands how you're feeling, it's me."

Grace looked up into Rebekah's eyes, the kindness she saw in them comforting. Someone actually did understand. "Thank you," she whispered, relief washing over her.

"You know, I think your trip sounds lovely," she mused. "As someone who has traveled the world, there are places I would love to show Thorne, but it might be nice to save that for another time and just focus on us for a change when it's time for our honeymoon." She looked at her watch, then grabbed her stuff. "Looks like it's time for the town council meeting. Are you ready?"

Grace startled at the abrupt change in topic, then quickly shook off her confusion and gathered her things. "I'm as ready as I'll ever be," she replied.

She followed Rebekah out to her car and climbed in. Now all she could do is hope the council is more receptive to her plans than the rest of the gang had been.

***

Grace and Rebekah walked into the meeting room and took a seat next to Molly. The room was a little less crowded this time—several of the council members missing, specifically Bea and Junior.

"Where's Bea and Junior?" Grace asked Molly.

Molly leaned closer. "Word on the street is she and Junior got into it, something about him not wanting to retire and her being ready to travel." Molly looked around to see if anyone was listening, then leaned even closer. "From what I heard, Bea got so frustrated she packed a bag and took off on her own."

"Are you serious?" Grace gasped. She knew Bea was looking forward to retirement and that Junior wasn't quite ready, but she never expected something like this!

After forty-plus years together, Grace just assumed they'd find a way to work things out. "That explains where Bea is, but where's Junior?" she asked, genuinely curious how he was holding up without Bea.

"He took off after her," Molly replied. "Austin and Tess are doing what they can to keep things running at the farm, but between Austin's job at the feed store—and Tess's job working for me—they're struggling."

That was a lot to take in. "Is there anything I can do to help?"

Molly shook her head. "You've got your own mountain to climb," she reminded Grace.

Mayor Allen entered the room and purposefully strode to the podium. "Good afternoon, everyone," he said to the crowd. "We've called this special meeting today to discuss Grace's newest event at the B&B. Grace, would you like to tell everyone about your plan?"

No matter how many times Grace did this, it never seemed to get easier. Some people were just not built for the spotlight, and she was one of them. She perched on the edge of her chair and addressed her fellow council members, who were all seated in a circle.

"I know everyone is expecting another Valentine's Day-themed event, but I think it would be so much more fun to host a Mardi Gras Experience!" she said, mustering up as much enthusiasm as possible for someone with a knot in their stomach the size of a watermelon. "It will start the Tuesday after next and run for one week, ending on Mardi Gras."

Addie raised a brow. "I must admit, I'm intrigued. I've never been to a Mardi Gras celebration. What exactly will this entail?"

Grace laid out her plans in as much detail as she could. When she was finished, she waited with bated breath for their response.

"I think it sounds like a ton of fun!" Lyda exclaimed. "I would love to do a booth at the carnival where I help people make Mardi Gras masks!"

God bless her, Grace loved that woman.

"It does sound fun," Addie mused. "But it also sounds like a ton of work. Do we really have time for this?"

Mayor Allen cleared his throat. "I'm sure we'll have no shortage of volunteers as soon as everyone hears about this exciting new plan!" He looked at Molly. "I trust you'll get the word out?"

Molly nodded. "The announcements are ready to go as soon as you say the word."

"Then I think it's settled," he declared.

"Wait a minute!" Addie interrupted. "Aren't we supposed to vote on this?"

A look of panic crossed his face so fast Grace wondered if she imagined it. What was going on? While she appreciated the fact he was supporting her and her plan, the council always voted on these things.

"Of course," he said, his smile returning. "I just want to remind everyone that these events tend to be very lucrative for the town, as well as for our small business owners."

Now Grace was certain something was wrong. She glanced at Molly, but her expression was a careful mask of indifference. She knew something.

"All in favor?" Mayor Allen asked.

Everyone raised their hands.

"All opposed?"

No hands raised.

"Good!" he exclaimed. "I'll see you all tomorrow morning at the kick-off meeting. I assume that will still be held at Addie's?"

"Of course," Addie assured him. "You know I'll be there!"

Mayor Allen nodded, a look of relief washing over his face. "Meeting adjourned."

With that, he was gone, the door swinging shut behind him.

"What's going on?" Grace asked Molly. "I know you know something," she chided. "Don't try to deny it."

Molly sighed. "Yes, I know something. But I'm not at liberty to discuss it at the moment."

A pang of hurt hit Grace in the stomach. "Even with us?" she asked, indicating herself and Rebekah.

"I'm sorry, but yes, even with you two," she said, her tone full of regret. "It's not personal," she was quick to assure them.

Grace searched Molly's face for a hint of what was going on, but found none. "It doesn't involve you or Grant, does it?" she asked, completely flabbergasted by this turn of events.

"No," Molly replied, "not in the way you're thinking anyway." She grabbed her purse and stood. "Look, I need to go. But I promise I will fill you in as soon as I'm able."

Before Grace could say anything else, Molly was gone, the door swinging behind her, just as it had Mayor Allen.

"That was weird," Grace said to Rebekah. She narrowed her eyes and studied her friend. "Do *you* know what's going on? Did I miss something while I was gone?"

Rebekah shook her head. "I'm just as much in the dark as you are." She gathered her things and stood. "Whatever it is, though, it must be big if Molly and Grant are involved."

"Why do you say that?" Grace asked as she followed Rebekah out of the building.

"I don't know," she said with a shrug. "It's just a feeling."

Grace considered what she was saying. She wanted to protest, but couldn't seem to come up with a reason why. Regardless, she'd been given the permission she needed to move forward with her plan. That meant it was go time! All hands on deck! Or, as they say in Louisiana: Laissez les bons temps rouler—let the good times roll

Days till Mardi Gras

-Eighteen-

G race got ready to go, then walked into the kitchen, wrapped her arms around Cole's waist, and buried her head in his shoulder. When he hugged her back, everything felt right with the world.

"What's wrong?" Cole asked. "You look...I don't know, melancholy?"

"I think I'm just going through some growing pains," she said, pulling back to look at him. "How about you? Have you settled back into your routine?"

A strange expression crossed his face, but he shrugged it off. "It's just like riding a bicycle," he replied.

"Now it's my turn to ask what's wrong," Grace said, studying him closely. Cole was usually a pretty easygoing guy, so if something was bothering him, that was a bad sign.

He remained silent for a moment, then shrugged again. "I'm sure it's nothing," he finally said. "Riley's been acting different since we got back. I tried asking him about it, but he made it clear he wasn't interested in talking."

Her natural inclination in this kind of situation would be to allow fear to take hold and push her into a panic attack, but she tried hard to keep that feeling at bay. "You don't think he plans to leave, do you?" she tried to ask casually.

Judging by the look he gave her, she did not succeed.

"I think that's a pretty rash conclusion to jump to," he drawled. He kissed her cheek, then whistled for the dogs, who studiously ignored him. "Guess they aren't ready to brave the weather just yet," he chuckled.

Grace laughed as she watched the dogs circle in their beds a couple of times, then lay down, their backs to Cole. "I think you're on your own for at least a few more weeks!" The smile left her face as her thoughts returned to Riley. "You should try to talk to him again," she encouraged. "If there is a problem, it would be best to get it under control sooner rather than later, don't you think?"

Cole shook his head. "As my old man used to say, let's not borrow trouble, okay?" He kissed her again, then headed for the door. "Let me know how the meeting goes," he called over his shoulder. And then he was gone.

***

Grace walked into Addie's, once again stunned to see it was standing-room only. Would she ever get used to this kind of turnout? She sincerely hoped not. She never wanted to reach a point when people's generosity became expected.

Molly and Rebekah were waiting for her at the back of the dining area, along with Mayor Allen. Speaking in front of a crowd was another thing she never seemed to get used to, and she wished either Molly or Rebekah would agree to do it for her. But no, they seemed content to let her be the spokesperson.

As she looked out at the sea of faces, she spotted Granny and Gladys sitting with Julian and Earl. That was a first. Out of all the meetings they'd held over the past year, neither of them had made it to a single one. It was a little jarring for Grace to see them now, though it did give her a bit of a confidence boost when they smiled and waved at her.

Mayor Allen clinked his glass with a spoon, then waited for the room to quiet down. "Good morning, everyone! Thank you all for coming out to, once again, support our town. We truly could not pull off these events without all of you." He beamed as the crowd clapped and cheered, then clinked his glass again. "Without further ado, I will turn the floor over to Grace so she can give you all the details." He stepped to the side, making room for Grace at the makeshift podium, which just so happened to be an old hostess stand.

Grace stepped forward and cleared her throat. "Thank you," she said to Mayor Allen. "This year we've decided to do something a little different and will be hosting Mardi Gras-themed events!" She went on to list them, her excitement building as the crowd oohed and aahed at each revelation. "So what I need from all of you are volunteers to decorate Main Street, volunteers to build parade floats, and volunteers to help set up for the Mayor's Masquerade

Ball. We also still have room for vendors at the carnival if anyone is interested in that."

There, she'd managed to make it through her speech without shaking too badly or losing her voice. Now all that was left was to get through the inevitable questions, and she would be on to the next problem.

"Aren't Mardi Gras parade floats really fancy?" a woman near the front asked. "How are we supposed to accomplish that in a week and a half?"

That was a great question. This wasn't the first time they'd thrown a parade together in this amount of time, but the other times had been Christmas-themed, which was significantly easier to pull off.

Rebekah stepped forward and smiled at Grace reassuringly. "To answer your question, yes, these floats can be a lot more involved than the ones we're used to, but I've already begun working with the art department at the high school, and we are confident we can put together something amazing. All we need is the manpower to do it."

"You mentioned a 5K charity run. Which charity will we be supporting, and who's in charge of that?" a man called out from the back.

"There is a non-profit in Kansas City that organizes and runs these," Grace explained. "And the charity we will be supporting is the March of Dimes." When no one else appeared to have any more questions, Grace continued, "Sign-up sheets are by the door. Thank you so much for your support—I truly do appreciate every single one of you."

She stepped back, Mayor Allen taking her place.

"Thank you all for showing up this morning! Don't forget to sign up on your way out, we'll see you again at the next check-in meeting!"

As soon as the crowd began to disperse, Grace walked over to Rebekah and Molly. "That went well."

"Yep," Rebekah agreed. She made some notes on a clipboard, then looked at Grace expectantly. "Any chance you're up for breakfast? And by up for it, I mean up for making it?"

Grace laughed, then nodded happily. This is exactly what she needs to get back in the swing of things—a return to her former routine! "Meet you at Granny's?"

When they nodded, she excused herself and made her way through the crowd. Never in her life had she been so excited to make breakfast before; she just hoped she still felt that way once she was back in the kitchen.

***

Grace let herself into the house, then made a beeline for the kitchen, stopping short when she saw Granny and Gladys had beat her there. "How did you two get back here so fast?"

Granny raised a brow over the rim of her mug as she took a sip of coffee. "Skill," she said as she took a seat next to Gladys at the breakfast bar.

"I could have used that skill over the last year myself," Grace joked as she entered the kitchen. "I was hoping to beat everyone to the kitchen today so I could get breakfast ready like I used to."

"If you want to cook, we won't stop you," Gladys quipped. "But you should know Josie and I have been meeting Julian and Earl over at Addie's for breakfast these last two weeks, and we plan to continue this new tradition of ours."

That was news to Grace. Both women had been at the table with the rest of the gang when she'd arrived the last two days. Although, now that she thought about it, they never did have plates in front of them. And that did explain why they were at the meeting this morning.

"We still show up for the others," Gladys explained, as if reading Grace's mind. "We like that tradition too."

Grace leaned over the counter and clasped her hands together. "There's a question I'd like to ask before the others get here," she said, piquing their curiosity, "do you by any chance know what's going on down at city hall?" She looked at Gladys specifically. If anyone knew what was going on, it was her. Not to mention, Molly and Grant do live with her. Grace wasn't saying Gladys is the type to eavesdrop...but she isn't *not* saying that either.

Gladys looked over her shoulder, then leaned forward toward Grace. "I may have overheard a thing or two," she said casually. "But I'm really not at liberty to say..."

It was Grace's turn to raise a brow. There may have been a lot of changes over the last few weeks, but Gladys's penchant for gossip wasn't one of them.

"Okay, fine, you didn't hear this from me, but while Derek was interim mayor, he discovered that someone has been embezzling funds from the city coffers."

Grace gasped, her hand going to her mouth. "But who would do such a thing?" It obviously wasn't Derek; it would make zero sense for him to tell on himself. And there's no way it could be Mayor Allen—he was the pastor of their church! She mentally went through the list of all the council members but couldn't imagine a single one of them stealing from the town. So who could it be?

"That part I don't know," Gladys said ruefully. "But I have my suspicions. I just hope I'm wrong," she said sadly.

With nothing left to do, Grace decided to get started on breakfast. Since it was her first day back, she decided she'd make her famous stuffed French toast with bacon, sausage, hash browns, and scrambled eggs. After all, why not get back in the swing of things with an artery-clogging breakfast fit for a queen? She'd just have to make sure to get in plenty of cardio later. She was certain there was something that needed to be cleaned somewhere—there always was.

She was just scooping the scrambled eggs into a serving dish when Molly and Grant appeared in the doorway.

"Something sure smells good in here!" Molly said enthusiastically. She set the baby carrier on a chair, then walked over to the breakfast bar and helped herself to the buffet Grace had laid out. "You have no idea how much we've missed your cooking!"

"I can second that!" Grant exclaimed as he joined Molly at the bar. "Not that we haven't appreciated Rebekah filling in for you," he added quickly.

Rebekah walked into the room and gave him a mock scowl. "I heard that," she said as she waited her turn to grab a plate. "Sheesh, I feed you guys cereal one time..."

"More like every other day," Emilio said as he entered the room. "Not that I was counting or anything."

"At least it was quality cereal," Rebekah grumbled.

Molly laughed, then gave Grace a mischievous smile. "I still remember the time Grace told me she burned a bowl of cereal!"

Grace's cheeks turned the same color as her hair. "I'm never going to live that down, am I?" she groaned.

"It's a testament to how far you've come," Molly said, bumping Grace's shoulder good-naturedly.

"And apparently how far I still have to go," Rebekah said, rolling her eyes. She draped an arm around Grace's shoulders. "In all seriousness, I too am glad to have you back."

They took their seats around the table, Granny and Gladys joining them.

"How are the guys?" Grace asked them. While she'd seen them at the meeting, she hadn't been close enough to do much more than wave.

Granny and Gladys exchanged a look.

"Doing well, though I'm not sure we can say the same about poor Austin and Tess," Gladys said with a shake of her head.

"Julian and Earl are helping as much as they can, but those two are drowning trying to keep Junior's farm afloat," Granny informed them.

Molly grimaced. "I think Tess is living solely on coffee and granola bars these days. We should consider inviting her to breakfast sometime, if for no other reason than she needs a hot meal."

Grace opened her mouth to point out they could have done that ages ago, then quickly shut it. It was completely possible Molly didn't like to fraternize with her employees, and it was not her place to interfere with that. "How about I send a plate for her with you this morning?" Grace offered. When Molly nodded, Grace turned to Gladys. "So what exactly is going on with Junior and Bea?"

Gladys waved her hand. "Oh, you know how it is. Bea's been talking for ages about retiring one day and traveling the country. Junior always agreed—likely to keep the peace—and then, when Bea up and announced it was finally time, Junior panicked."

"What does that mean?" Grace asked, her brow furrowed as she tried to picture the turn of events.

"Simply put, the old coot ain't ready to give up the farm!" Granny exclaimed. She shook her head. "The only way a farmer retires is when he's six feet under."

Rebekah made a tsking sound. "You sound like you're talking from experience," she mused. "Or is this a warning to a certain someone?" she asked, nodding toward Grace.

"Both," Granny replied. "I've been trying to convince Julian to at least hire some help out at his farm. The only time I get to see him is in the morning for breakfast and occasionally in the evenings. I wouldn't mind seeing a few places myself before my time is up, but he's always got an excuse."

Grace wanted to assure Granny she had plenty of time, but she knew better. Had she made a mistake in reuniting Granny and Julian? She had wanted Granny to have someone to share the rest of her years with, not saddle her with someone who didn't have time for her.

"Don't you go getting ideas in that pretty little head of yours!" Granny admonished as she reached over and patted Grace's hand. "Julian and I will sort out our business ourselves."

"Am I that obvious?" Grace asked sheepishly.

When everyone nodded, she blushed again. Desperate to change the subject, she decided to grill Molly and Grant and see if she could get one of them to slip up and reveal the name of the person who was caught stealing.

"So, Mayor Allen sure was acting strange at the council meeting yesterday," Grace said to Molly. She elbowed Rebekah and tried to telepathically communicate with her to follow along.

"Oh, um, I thought so too," Rebekah said between bites of bacon.

Grace side-eyed her but continued. "You have any idea why that is?" Grace asked.

Molly wiped her mouth with a napkin, then pushed her chair back. "Sorry, guys, I need to get to work."

Grant folded his newspaper and followed suit. "Me too," he replied, grabbing the car seat and making a beeline for the door.

"Wait!" Grace called out, rushing after Molly. "You forgot about breakfast for Tess."

"I'll grab her a breakfast sandwich from Addie's," Molly called back as she closed the front door.

Grace returned to her seat. "She could have at least come up with an excuse that made sense," she muttered. Her head popped up as an idea formed. "I know, I'll bring lunch down to their office later today. Molly won't be able to get away from me there!"

"Don't bother," Gladys said, shaking her head. "I already tried that trick twice!"

It was a little surprising to see Gladys give up so easily, but Grace supposed she would find out eventually. Not that she was anxious to see someone she knows get in trouble. In fact, that was the last thing she wanted. For now, she would just hope it was all a misunderstanding.

"What should we do today?" she asked, changing the subject for the second time. "It's a little early to start cleaning for the guests, though I suppose we should start thinking about a menu. Since we're doing a Mardi Gras theme, I figure we should focus on Cajun and French cuisines. I'm looking forward to trying out new recipes."

Rebekah pushed her chair back and stood. "I'm happy to be a taste tester, but if this morning is any indication, I think you can officially count me out as your sous chef!"

"I'll take you up on that offer," Grace replied as she cleared the plates. "You're the only one I know who's snobby enough to have those types of food!"

"I think you mean cultured enough," Rebekah sniffed.

They eyed each other for a moment, then burst into laughter.

"Don't count us out," Granny called out. "We might not be cultured, but we know good food when we eat it!"

"Alright then, it's settled," Grace replied. "Today my training as a Cajun chef officially begins!"

Days till Mardi Gras

-Seventeen-

While it was true there were still seventeen days till Mardi Gras, there were only about half that until the guests arrived—assuming she had guests. But there was no reason to think she wouldn't, was there? Grace shook off her doubts; of course there wasn't. Despite the naysayers, she had no reason to believe people would love this experience any less than the other ones she'd hosted over the last year. In fact, this would be the biggest and best one yet!

Now with that little pep talk out of the way, she walked up to Lyda's porch and rang the bell, grinning when she heard the sound of feet pounding as Colton and Weston raced to the door.

"Hey guys!" she exclaimed, her greeting going unnoticed as the two rambunctious boys fought over the door.

Lyda appeared, her eyes rolling as she took in the sight. "Cookies are on the table!" she said loudly.

Grace watched in fascination as the boys immediately quit wrestling over the door and rushed off toward the kitchen.

"You look like someone who just got a glimpse of their future and is terrified of what they saw," Lyda teased. She pulled Grace into a hug. "Welcome home!"

"Thanks," Grace replied, returning the hug. "It's good to be back."

They walked inside, Lyda leading the way to the kitchen. "Is it?" she asked, her brow raised. "You're telling me you would rather be here than off somewhere with that handsome husband of yours?"

"That does sound nice," Grace said, a smile automatically crossing her lips anytime Cole was mentioned. "But it's also nice to see everyone again. And believe it or not, I am looking forward to hosting another event! Which brings me to why I'm here."

"Awesome!" she exclaimed, passing Grace a plate of cookies as she indicated a chair. "I've been hoping I might get to play a part in this. Mardi Gras is one of my absolute favorite holidays!"

That was music to Grace's ears. "I'm glad to hear that," Grace said as she bit into the cookie. "These are great! Family recipe?"

"Pssh, girl, ain't nobody got time for that. These came out of a tube from the store." She waved her hand dismissively. "But enough about that, what do you need from me?"

"I came to see if you're still interested in setting up a booth at the carnival. I believe you mentioned helping people make masks at the council meeting, but I was hoping you might have some to sell as well for those who'd rather buy something ready-made. The Mayor's Ball is going to be a masquerade ball, so I want people to have ample opportunities to acquire a mask," Grace explained.

Lyda nodded. "I think I missed the part about the masquerade ball, but it sounds great to me! I'll take any excuse to dress up!" Her smile turned into a frown. "This means I need to find a date, doesn't it?"

Grace opened her mouth to protest—to remind her friend that she didn't need a man to have fun—but then she thought better of it. That was easy to say when you had a husband and you weren't the only one in your friend group without a partner. "Let's not worry about that right now. There's still a couple of weeks until the ball, and between my guests and all the people sure to come here for the festivities, you could find yourself with more men than you know what to do with!"

"You know that's one thing I've always appreciated about you," Lyda said, her lips pursed. "You're an eternal optimist."

That didn't quite sound like a compliment, but Grace decided to go with it. If that was her biggest crime, so be it. "Anyway, I would like you to do a private mask-building workshop with my guests. I don't want to leave it to chance that all of them will visit your booth during the carnival."

"I would love that! Just tell me when and where and I'll be there!"

"I still need to work the details out with Rebekah, but I'll get back to you on that ASAP," Grace said as she pushed back her chair and stood to leave. "Let me know if you need money in advance to buy supplies."

Lyda nodded. "It wouldn't hurt," she said absentmindedly. She turned her focus back to Grace. "Would it be okay if I had some of my hats for sale in the booth? I have some that would go well with the masks. Plus, it's just a slow time of year, you know?"

"I don't have a problem with that," Grace replied. "Sell as many as you want; it's your booth."

As they walked to the foyer, the boys were nowhere to be seen—or heard. Lyda paused when they reached the door.

"Hey, what's going on down at city hall?" Lyda asked. She leaned back against the wall and crossed her arms. "There is no way you don't know something by now, seeing as how you spend so much time with those who are likely to know."

Grace felt like a deer in the headlights. Yes, she'd heard some gossip, but as of now, that's all it was. The last thing she wanted to do was be responsible for spreading that gossip.

"I asked Molly, but she refused to confirm or deny anything," Grace replied. That wasn't actually true. Molly had all but confirmed something was going on with her abrupt departure the day before at breakfast, but Grace wasn't about to admit that.

Lyda looked skeptical. "You're not holding out on me, are you?"

It wasn't easy, but Grace managed to maintain eye contact. "I swear if I knew something, I would tell you," she replied carefully, only half lying. "But you're a member of the council too. If there really is something going on, I'm sure you'll find out as soon as I do."

"I suppose you're right," Lyda reluctantly agreed. "I just want to feel included, that's all. It's hard fitting in in a new town. Especially these small towns where everyone knows everyone. I keep hoping once my store finally opens I'll start to feel more like a part of the community, but that little project is moving slower than dirt!"

Grace could understand her frustration. She loved her community and the part she played in it, and could see how it would be hard to feel like an outsider. Especially since this had been Lyda's home once before. Coming back to a place she grew up in and feeling like she didn't fit in must be more painful than simply starting over somewhere new. Grace would have to try harder to make her feel more welcome and a part of things.

"If you need any help on that front, let me know," Grace told her. "I'm sure we can organize a volunteer committee to help you get things going. People love to help, and I'm sure they'll be even more willing when they hear you're doing this for your grandmother."

"I appreciate that," Lyda replied, her expression doubtful. "But if you had any idea what I'm dealing with, you would walk that back in a heartbeat!"

Her phone rang, the caller ID showing Granny's name. "I better take this," Grace said apologetically. "I'll get back to you ASAP!" She walked outside to her car and pressed the answer button. "Hi, Granny."

"Hi, Grace, are you on your way back to the house?"

"No, but I can be there in a couple of minutes. Is everything okay?"

"Yes, dear. But there's someone here to see you, and I need to get going, so…"

That was news to her. She hadn't been expecting anyone, nor did she think it was possible for any guests to arrive early. As far as she knew, they didn't even have any booked yet. Though, with her luck, she wouldn't be surprised if that had changed and no one had bothered to tell her.

She sighed inwardly, then started the car. "I'll be right there."

***

When Grace got back to the B&B, a familiar car was parked in front of the house. Curious as to what would bring Evie here unannounced, Grace hurried inside, immediately regretting that decision.

"Please don't hate me," Evie pleaded. She gave Grace a puppy dog look, her hands clasped together in front of her and raised to her chest.

"Why would she hate you?" Shelley asked, a bored expression on her face.

Grace closed her eyes diand blew out her breath. She already knew where this was going, and she briefly considered fleeing back the way she'd come. Since she knew that wouldn't be fair to everyone else, she opened her eyes and studied Shelley. Other than the cast on her left arm, she looked exactly the same as she had last

Halloween—down to the haughty look she was giving Grace.

"I see nothing's changed around here," Shelley snarked. "Same boring town, same boring people."

"Why are you here?" Grace blurted. She could feel the tension building in her temples and knew a headache was sure to follow.

Evie cleared her throat. "As you can see, Shelley is injured," Evie explained, motioning to her arm, "and she needs a place to stay while she recovers."

"Do I want to know why you thought this would be a good place for that?"

Shelley snorted. "Our loser parents are still mad about me making them 'look bad'," she said, making air quotes with her good hand. "And Evie claims her cabin is too small, so..."

Grace was about to suggest a hotel when it dawned on her that she was the one who owned the only hotel in town. Drat! Was it too late to go back on her honeymoon?

"Our parents have agreed to pay as much as it will take for you to agree to let her stay," Evie offered. "They just don't want people to know about it, if you catch my drift."

Oh, Grace caught it, all right. She'd be embarrassed too after everything Shelley had done—too bad the one who should be embarrassed wasn't at all. In fact, as far as Grace could tell, Shelley didn't think she'd done a single thing wrong. It was hard to fathom that level of unawareness, but that was Shelley in a nutshell.

"What happened to your arm?" Grace asked, genuinely curious.

"She broke onto a movie set and attempted to do a stunt, failed spectacularly, then broke her arm, a stuntwoman's leg, and the nose of the lead actor," Evie said dryly. She shook her head. "They're threatening to sue, and I'm pretty sure the only reason they haven't is because she's flat broke. She has been blacklisted from every film studio in the world, though, so I suppose that's an accomplishment of some kind."

Shelley rolled her eyes. "You make it sound so booorrringgg," she dragged out the syllables, dramatically enunciating each one. "So, it's like this. They were filming a scene for one of those superhero movies, and I just knew I would make a better stunt double than the loser they picked. I mean, come on, have you seen my social media account? I'm up to over a million followers, and that woman has barely ten thousand!"

She paused to take a breath, then continued. "Anyway, I figured all I had to do was show them what they were missing and they'd fire her in an instant and hire me! So, I pretended to work for the catering company, snuck on set, then hooked myself up to one of the harnesses they had just dangling there. What I didn't know was that the harness was connected to a set of sandbags, and once I added my weight to it, all heck broke loose. I mean, how was I supposed to know?" she scoffed. "I do all my own stunts live, no equipment necessary."

Grace still had nightmares about Shelley's 'stunts', so she had no problem imagining the chaos that ensued. The thing that most concerned her was the blacklisted part. "If Shelley's been blacklisted, what's she going to do once her arm heals?" Grace was almost afraid to hear the answer. Surely her parents didn't expect her to stay with Grace indefinitely? Although, knowing them, she wouldn't be surprised if that's exactly what they expected.

"We're still working out those details," Evie said cryptically. "For now, we just need to put her somewhere where she can rest and, well, stay out of trouble."

The last thing Grace wanted was to be responsible for keeping Shelley out of trouble. Was that even possible? She sure didn't think so. "I can give her a room at the hotel," Grace reluctantly offered. "Aside from the carnival crew, who are checking in late next week, Shelley will have the place to herself."

"Carnival crew?" Shelley's eyes lit up. "Why didn't you tell me a carnival was coming to town? This is great news!"

Don't ask, don't ask, don't ask, Grace willed herself. "Why is that great news?" Grace asked, wincing as she prepared for what was sure to be an insane answer.

"Duh! Don't carnivals have acts? Tightrope walkers, men who swallow swords, a bearded lady? With my talent, I'm sure to become their number one star!"

"I think those are circus acts," Grace mused. "Besides that, you're not in any shape to perform, remember?" Grace nodded toward Shelley's cast.

Shelley let out an unladylike snort. "No way I'm letting this old thing come between me and my big break," she said, waving the cast around. "Now give me my room key so I can get out of here. I need to go give my fans the good news, and you guys are killing the vibe."

'I am so sorry,' Evie mouthed.

Getting Shelley out there was more than fine with Grace, so she turned back toward the door and motioned for them to follow. One thing was for sure: the hotel rate just doubled—no, make that tripled! Oh, who was she kidding? Was there any amount of money that would make the chaos that was sure to follow worth it?

-Sixteen-

The day Grace had been waiting for finally arrived, Sunday! It was the one day a week she and Cole had agreed would be their official day to spend together. No work, no obligations, unless of course she had guests—just them. And church, but that didn't count as work or an obligation.

Since Cole was taking Sunday off, and the animals still had to be fed, he and Riley had decided to alternate days so each of them could have a full day off—Cole had Sunday, Riley had Saturday. An arrangement Grace felt was hard won, and she was desperate not to lose it. Which is why, instead of enjoying her morning with her new husband, she was now pestering him about the Riley situation.

"Did you talk to Riley?" she asked, dropping down on the sofa next to Cole and cuddling close. Piper took that as her cue to join them and plopped down in Grace's lap.

Cole eyed her over the rim of his coffee cup. "What was I supposed to talk to him about?"

Grace rolled her eyes. Men! Always so stubborn. "You were supposed to talk to him about why he was acting weird," she reminded him.

"If I had known that comment would set off a firestorm in you, I never would have mentioned it," Cole drawled. He wrapped his arm around her shoulder and kissed the top of her head. "You worry too much, darlin'."

She leaned over to look up at him. "I very much disagree, sir. Riley is the only thing standing between you having time off and you working yourself into an early grave, so his happiness, job satisfaction, or whatever else he needs to stick around should be of the utmost concern—to both of us."

"I suppose you have a point," he conceded. "But he hasn't said anything that would indicate there's a problem, and other than offering to lend an ear if he needs one, what would you have me do? Lasso him to a chair and refuse to let him go until he shares his feelings?"

Grace's eyes widened. "You can do that?"

"No!" he said with a laugh. "Honey, seriously, you need to let this go. This is supposed to be our day, and the last thing I want to do is spend it worrying about things that are out of our control."

He had a point, so she decided to let it go—for now. "Shelley's back," she announced, thoroughly enjoying the look of surprise on Cole's face as he worked to avoid spitting out his coffee.

"Do I want to know?" he choked out. He coughed a few times as the coffee went down the wrong pipe.

Concerned, Grace took his cup and set it on the table, then rubbed his back. "I expected you to be surprised; I didn't expect the news to kill you," she teased. "And no, you don't want to know why any more than you want to know that she's staying at the hotel for the foreseeable future."

Cole groaned. "Why?" he asked, his hand raking down his face. "You know there is absolutely zero good that can come from this, right?"

Boy, did she know. She'd been responsible for keeping Shelley out of trouble last Halloween and had had the privilege more than once of stopping her from doing something reckless and stupid. And Shelley wasn't even staying at the hotel that time! For all Grace knew, when she went to check on her later she'd find a zipline running from the roof to the bar across the street, or worse, there'd be a parkour course in the dining room. Grace shuddered at the thought.

"Evie practically begged me," she replied. "What was I supposed to do?"

"You don't have to say yes every time someone asks you to do something," he said through gritted teeth. "No is an acceptable answer."

"Shelley's parents are paying triple our normal fee per night," Grace informed him, hopeful that would be enough to soothe his ruffled feathers. She didn't blame him for being irritated; he'd had to kick Shelley off his farm when she snuck on to perform one of her 'stunts,' and Grace knew that still bothered him. Especially since Shelley had almost been trampled by one of his bulls.

He shook his head and reached over to grab his coffee. "I don't think there's enough money in this world to justify having her around."

Hadn't that been Grace's exact thought yesterday? But it had simply never occurred to her to say no. Evie was her friend—how do you say no to a friend? Although, now that she was married, maybe this was one of those things she should discuss with Cole first? After all, her problems could easily become his problems, especially financial ones.

"I'm sorry," she said softly. "Yes, Shelley is annoying, but I didn't think it would be that big of a deal to let her stay at the hotel; it's not like she's moving into Granny's." Grace sighed. "I should have talked to you first."

Cole reached over and pulled her close. "It's okay," he assured her. "I'm not happy about it, but I understand how hard it is for you to pass on an opportunity to help the people you care about."

"What's the worst that can happen?" Grace asked, knowing full well she was tempting fate by even asking.

"Let's see," Cole said, holding up his finger. "She could perform some crazy stunt at the hotel, get hurt, then sue you." He held up a second finger. "She could trash the place and cause a ton of damage that could cost a fortune to repair." He held up his third finger. "And worst of all, she could drive you crazy with demands and rob you of your peace and happiness. To be honest, my money is on number three, but you never know with her—she could throw us a curveball and do them all."

All of that sounded bad and left Grace regretting the moment she chose to go back to the house yesterday. If she'd gone back to the farm instead, Evie would have asked someone else, and it would have been up to them to tell her no. And literally everyone else would have likely said no and had no problem doing so. Why was she always such a pushover? Regardless, it was done now, so nothing left to do but try to minimize the fallout.

***

Since it was a surprisingly warm day for February, Grace, Cole, Granny, and Julian decided to go back to Granny's after church for an impromptu BBQ. Grace and Cole stopped by the local store for steak and chicken, Grace grabbing an extra can of baked beans and a container of cole slaw, just in case they'd run out while she was gone. She still needed to stock up on groceries for the B&B before her guests arrived—guests she still wasn't sure were coming since Molly hadn't given an update on that front yet.

When they got back to the house, Cole and Julian migrated toward the deck to get the grill fired up while Grace and Granny busied themselves in the kitchen preparing the meat and sides.

"You and Julian seem to be getting along pretty well," Grace mused out loud. "Might there be another wedding in our future?"

Granny tsked. "It's only been three weeks since you got married, child. Don't you think that's a little soon for happily ever after?"

"If you'd just met, I'd say yes," Grace replied, "but he was your first love, and you've known each other most of your lives, so..."

"He was my first love almost seventy years ago," Granny reminded her. "And we've avoided each other ever since we had that falling out." Granny shook her head. "We aren't the same people we were back then. Not to mention, his children aren't quite as keen on our new relationship as you seem to be."

Grace stopped stirring the beans and turned to face Granny, her hands on her hips. "Are you telling me his kids, who are at least sixty, are giving him grief about you? For Pete's sake, you'd think they'd be thrilled their dad has found someone to spend his golden years with."

Granny continued arranging cheese, pickles, olives, and crackers on a platter, her trembling hands the only indication she was upset. "He was married to their mother for most of their lives. It's not surprising at all they would have a difficult time seeing their dad with someone else. I'm sure they'll come around eventually."

"But Granny—" Grace paused, unsure of how to proceed without being offensive. "I don't mean to be rude, but you two aren't getting any younger. I'm not sure you have time to waste waiting around on something that may not happen."

"That's what I've been telling her," Julian said as he approached the breakfast bar. "But this one is as stubborn as the day is long."

"So that's where Grace gets her stubborn streak," Cole teased as he walked up beside Julian. "The grill is ready if you are," Cole told Grace.

Grace handed him a platter of seasoned meat, then waited for the two men to return to the deck before she continued. "If even Julian thinks the kids—and I use that term loosely—are being unreasonable, then what's the real issue?"

She was silent so long, Grace was sure she wasn't going to answer.

"Us old people are stuck in our ways," Granny finally replied. Her tone held a slight edge to it as she made it clear she did not want to have this conversation. "Julian isn't ready to sell the farm, and I have no desire to leave the only home I've ever known unless it's in a body bag, so how do we navigate that?" She shook her head. "There are just too many unanswered questions at this point to even consider the possibility of a future together. Besides, I'm enjoying things as they are. It's nice to have someone to do things with, and if that's all that ever comes of this, it'll be fine by me."

The men returned a second time, unknowingly providing Granny a temporary reprieve from Grace's meddling. And she did mean temporary. This wasn't over, not by a long shot. Grace knew how much Granny still loved Julian and was not about to allow something so trivial to come between them. After all, she and Cole had had the same problem, and they managed to work it out. Granny and Julian could do the same.

As Grace handed each of them a glass of iced tea, the front door burst open, startling her so much her tea sloshed out of the glass and all over the counter.

"What on earth!" Grace exclaimed as all eyes turned to see who had caused such a ruckus.

The sight of Shelley storming toward her caused Grace to groan, then groan again as Cole shot her an 'I told you so' glance.

"There you are!" Shelley yelled, the finger on her good hand pointing at Grace accusatorily. "Where have you been? I've been waiting for my breakfast for hours!"

That was news to Grace. At no point did she remember offering to provide meals. Although, now that she thought about it, how was Shelley supposed to feed herself? As far as Grace knew, she didn't have a car, and the rooms at the hotel didn't provide much beyond a coffee maker and microwave. How did she keep getting herself into these messes?

"I'm sorry, Shelley, I didn't know you were expecting breakfast," Grace said lamely.

"All. Hotels. Offer. Breakfast." Shelley enunciated. "What do you think my parents are paying you for?"

Grace took a deep breath as she avoided looking at Cole. She didn't have to see him to know his lips were twitching as he watched the very thing he'd warned her about that morning happen in real time. "I assumed they were paying for your room," Grace replied with as much authority as she could muster.

"Pfftt, for that kind of money, I could stay at an all-inclusive resort," she retorted.

"So why don't you?" Grace shot back.

Tears filled Shelley's eyes, big dramatic drops rolling down her cheeks. "I was so scared when I got hurt," she sniffled, "that all I wanted to do was come home and be with my mom. But she doesn't want me, and now I'm stuck here with nowhere to go and no way to get there."

Guilt immediately washed over Grace until she saw Shelley peek up at her to see if her little con was working. "You almost had me," Grace told her. "Honestly, I think you missed your calling as an actress. If you had tried acting instead of stunt work, you might have been successful."

Shelley perked up. "You really think so?"

"Sure," Grace replied, hopeful this wouldn't come back to bite her in the butt someday. "But for now, why don't you join us for lunch? We can figure out meals while we eat."

"You had me at lunch," Shelley replied. She rushed across the room, grabbed a plate, and filled it as high as she could with the hors d'oeuvres Granny had set out.

They watched in silence as she stuffed as much food as she could in her mouth, little cracker crumbs flying everywhere as she chewed. Why she didn't just grab the platter was anyone's guess, since she all but emptied it.

"I'll make some more," Granny said, turning toward the fridge.

"I'll help," Grace said, following close behind.

Completely oblivious to their discomfort, Shelley took a seat at the table and continued to munch away.

"This is not the nice lunch I was hoping for," Grace whispered to Granny. "What are we going to do about her?"

Granny shrugged. "Treat her the same as we would any other guest."

"Okay, that works for now, but what about the rest of the time? Surely you don't want a repeat of this every time you sit down for a meal?"

"Aren't you opening the hotel up for the carnival workers?" Granny asked, as if the solution to the problem was obvious.

While it was true she had agreed to do that to make it easier on the workers, she hadn't expected to provide three meals a day like she did for her usual guests. Was that a mistake? She would have to remember to talk to Rebekah and Molly about that.

"I'll figure something out," Grace muttered.

Thankfully, the men chose that moment to return to the table with the now fully cooked meat, which gave Grace something else to focus on for the time being. Maybe the meal could be saved after all. She watched Shelley plop half the meat on her now-empty plate. Then again, maybe not.

-Fifteen-

This time when the breakfast gang assembled, there was excitement in the air. It had been a long time since they'd planned an event together, the last time being in early December when they planned the Christmas Experience. In her opinion, her wedding didn't count, and the New Year's Eve Anniversary Party happened so quickly they pulled that one off on nothing more than a wing and a prayer. Grace had to admit, she was really looking forward to this one, it being so different from the other events she'd hosted.

"Do I want to know why you cooked so much food?" Molly asked as she passed around the huge serving dish of gumbo.

Grace held back a sigh. "I plan to take the leftovers to Shelley when we're finished," she explained. "I don't know how she managed it, but when she was here yesterday she ate so much food the rest of us were left fighting for scraps."

Molly raised one perfectly manicured brow. "It must be all those stunts she performs."

"You think she's still filming videos?" Grace asked—she slapped her forehead with her palm. "Of course she's still filming videos. This is Shelley we're talking about! There's no way she would go a single day without posting content for her 'adoring fans.'"

"More like rabid fans," Rebekah replied as she turned her phone screen so Grace and Molly could see it.

They watched in morbid fascination as a video of Shelley attempting to ride a skateboard down a flight of stairs, cast and all, played in front of them. A series of "Do it!" flooded the comments section below the video as her fans encouraged her nonsense with reckless abandon.

"Wait a minute," Grace said, peering closer at the screen. "Are those the stairs at the hotel?" She searched for the date the video was posted and saw it was yesterday. "Oh my gosh, it *is* the stairs at the hotel!" She watched in horror as Shelley made it halfway, lost her balance, then somersaulted the rest of the way down. When she reached the bottom, she lay there for a moment, then popped up, threw her good arm in the air 'Tiny Tim style,' then bowed dramatically. "She's insane," Grace whispered.

Emilio cleared his throat. "I hate to be the one to point this out, but do you really think it's wise to give her free rein of the hotel? You know this kind of behavior is going to continue, and at some point, she *will* hurt herself."

"I agree with Emilio," Grant chimed in as he folded his newspaper and set it down on the table beside his plate. "I know you don't want to hear this, Grace, but I think Shelley needs to move here where there are people to keep an eye on her."

"But what about my guests?" she sputtered. She turned to Molly, a panicked look in her eyes. "We do have guests coming, right?"

Molly placed a calming hand on Grace's arm. "Yes, silly, half the rooms have already been booked, and there are still a few more potential guests waiting on my approval."

"So then where would she stay?" Grace asked. She knew the answer but could not bring herself to say it out loud.

"She could take my room," Rebekah volunteered. "I can go stay at the hotel until the event is over and things calm down. I'm sure it wouldn't hurt to have one of us there while the workers stay anyway."

If Grace had been sitting next to Rebekah, she would have hugged her. She knew Rebekah was only volunteering so Grace wouldn't have to give Shelley her bedroom, and it meant the world to her that her friend understood how hard that would be. It also made her feel awful to kick Rebekah out of her room. Grace knew Rebekah had had a hard time feeling settled here, and she didn't want to do anything to give her the impression that it would be easy to pack up and move so easily.

"Or you could take my room," Grace blurted out before she could think better of it. "I should have offered that before I left on my honeymoon."

"But then where would you stay while the guests are here?" Molly asked Grace. "Weren't you planning to be here in case someone needed something during the night?"

Grace had expected that and was already one step ahead of them. "If Rebekah stays here, she can take my place and help out if someone needs something."

"Oh no," Rebekah said, shaking her head. "You are not leaving me here to deal with Shelley and her shenanigans, which you just know are going to be bad. *I'm* going to the hotel, *you're* staying here, and we're all going to be happy. Well, except for Shelley, who I have a feeling is not going to like this change in plans."

That would likely be the understatement of the century. No matter how Grace chose to phrase the 'request,' going from the freedom of the hotel to the confinement of the house would likely feel like going to prison. But maybe that would motivate Shelley to get her act together quicker. One could only hope.

"I'll go break the news," Grace sighed, pushing back her chair. "So much for our big planning session this morning."

"Tomorrow works better for me anyway," Molly said as she joined Grace in clearing the plates. "I should have the final guest list by then so we'll know exactly who and what we're working with."

It was hard to argue with that, so Grace finished cleaning up and headed out. As long as both Shelley and the hotel were still in one piece by the time she got there, she would consider that a win. Anything after that would be icing on the cake.

***

"Absolutely not!" Shelley shouted at Grace. "I am not moving to your boring house so you can babysit me like I'm some kind of child!"

"If you didn't act like a child, I wouldn't have to make you move!" Grace yelled back. She took a deep breath and willed herself to calm down. Matching Shelley's energy would get her nowhere. "Weren't you the one who said you'd rather stay at the house anyway?"

Shelley considered that for a moment, then shrugged. "I've changed my mind."

More like discovered all the reckless stunts she could pull with no one around to stop her. "If you come to the house, you'll never miss a meal again," Grace said sweetly, fingers crossed her bribe would work.

"You already promised to bring me food," Shelley countered.

Is this what it felt like to reason with a toddler? Because that's how it felt. "But we're going to have tons of activities at the house once the guests are there," Grace tried again. "I'm sure you'll find plenty of opportunities to film content for your followers."

She narrowed her eyes, then in a shocking turn of events, gave in. "Okay, fine, you win. Give me fifteen minutes to pack and I'll be ready to go."

Grace's mouth gaped open momentarily, then shut just as quickly as she scrambled to get out of there before Shelley changed her mind. As she waited in the lobby, she began to pace, her fear growing with each step. Why had Shelley changed her mind? What did she have planned? Images of Shelley trying to ski off the widow's walk flashed through her mind. There had to be something she could do to fix this.

If real life were a comic strip, a light bulb would be flashing over Grace's head as the perfect solution came to her. She had to be careful. If Shelley had even the tiniest inkling Grace was trying to manipulate her, she would dig her heels in that much harder.

"My bags are packed and ready to go," Shelley announced as she entered the lobby.

"Where are they?" Grace asked, looking pointedly at Shelley's empty hands.

Shelley rolled her eyes and huffed. "In my room, duh. How do you expect me to carry them with a broken arm?"

Only one of her arms was broken, but Grace decided this was not a battle worth fighting. Without a word, she went to Shelley's room, retrieved the luggage, then made her way back to the lobby, where she found Shelley filming an update for her followers.

"This here is the mean lady taking away all our fun," she said, turning the camera on her phone toward Grace.

Grace quickly dropped a suitcase and covered her face. "You can't film me without permission!" she shrieked.

Shelley turned the phone back to her. "See, total stick in the mud. But fear not, adoring fans, I have plans so cool they'll make my previous videos look like child's play. See you soon!" She blew a kiss at the camera, then turned it off and turned toward Grace. "You really need to lighten up. Imagine the publicity I could bring you if you'd let me feature you in some of my videos. You could be the Mr. Dithers to my Dagwood Bumstead."

"I am honestly shocked you know who that is," Grace said dryly. "Regardless, I am not interested in appearing in your videos. After all, I'm not an actress..." She picked the suitcase up and began walking toward the door, anxious to see if Shelley would take the hint.

"But you don't have to be an actress," Shelley said, falling into step beside Grace. "I'm not."

Grace stopped walking and gave Shelley an open-mouthed stare. "Really? I thought we discussed the other day that you were an actress? Didn't we talk about how good you are?" Grace tried to give the impression she was searching her memories, whatever that looked like. "I could have sworn someone said you'd be perfect in a sitcom."

"I mean, I don't remember that, but now that you mention it, I would be perfect, wouldn't I?"

"Oh, absolutely," Grace said, nodding enthusiastically. "You could be the next Lucille Ball!" She sent a silent apology to Ms. Ball, praying she would understand. And who knows, maybe Shelley really would make a great comedic actress. She hadn't been half bad when she'd played the part of the ghost woman haunting the hotel last Halloween.

Shelley hopped in the passenger seat while Grace loaded her suitcases into the trunk. When Grace joined her a moment later, she was deep in thought. "You know, I think you're right. This whole 'stunt-woman' thing didn't exactly work out as planned, and I bet that's because my real calling is to be an actress. From now on, I'm going to focus on showing the world my talent, starting with my campaign to become the Mardi Gras Queen!"

Grace's head whipped toward Shelley so fast, she feared she gave herself whiplash. "What do you mean by Mardi Gras Queen?"

"Isn't there going to be a parade?" Shelley asked.

"Yes," Grace said, her eyes closing as she mentally prepared herself for the insanity she knew was coming.

"And won't there be a dance at the end?"

"Yes," Grace replied, still unsure how this translated to Mardi Gras Queen.

"Duh! That calls for a queen! And a king, but I don't care about that." She gave Grace the side-eye. "As long as it isn't Greg. I'm still mad at him for leaving town last July and not taking me with him."

If Greg was out of town, how could he be the king? was a question Grace would have asked if she wasn't still trying to figure out where this business about a queen came from. Then it hit her. "Wait, are you thinking about a homecoming queen?"

"Same difference," Shelley replied.

"What does that have to do with—never mind," Grace said as she pulled into the driveway. All that mattered was Shelley was no longer intent on performing stunts. She was sure she should be concerned about this newest plan, but campaigning for a title that didn't exist seemed harmless enough. In fact, if it kept Shelley busy, Grace would willingly crown her herself. "Let's get you inside and settled into your new room," Grace said, changing the subject.

When they reached Rebekah's room, Grace took a look around, terrified to see the room looked exactly as it had a year ago—before Rebekah moved in. In fact, there wasn't a single piece of evidence to suggest anyone had ever lived there. No photos on the nightstand, no keepsakes or mementos on the top of the dresser. How had Rebekah managed to pack so quickly? Or was it more likely she'd never fully unpacked in the first place?

Shelley wrinkled her nose. "This room is smaller than my closet at home."

Grace's room didn't even have a closet. "I'm sure you'll spend most of your time outside of the room anyway," she reassured her. "After all, you can't run a campaign from your bedroom." Why was she encouraging her?

"Fine," Shelley shrugged. She flung herself onto the bed, then turned to Grace expectantly. "I'll take my breakfast now."

Taken aback by the sudden change in demeanor, Grace stared blankly for a moment. "We usually eat breakfast around seven thirty, but there are plenty of leftovers downstairs. Feel free to help yourself." She turned to leave, then stopped when Shelley called her back.

"Is this not a bed and breakfast?" Shelley asked.

"Yes," Grace replied reluctantly.

"Well," Shelley pointed to the bed. "Bed and breakfast." She made the sign for eating from a plate, her eyes rolling as if Grace were the dense one.

"That's not—" Grace buried her face in her hands and sighed. "You know what, fine. Stay here, I'll bring your food up right away, miss."

This was the last thing Grace intended to do today, but sometimes desperate times called for desperate measures. And no doubt about it, she was desperate to keep Shelley in line, whatever that took.

As she took the stairs two at a time, Cole's words from the other day echoed through her mind. Yes, she should have said no when Evie begged her to take Shelley off her hands. Yes, she did regret her decision. But she was in it now—nothing left to do but try to make the best of it.

-Fourteen-

"Is it finally time to talk about our guests?" Grace asked once everyone was seated at the table. She wasn't about to admit it, but she was anxious to get out of there. Shelley had been driving her nuts non-stop since she got there, and for once, Grace wanted her to be someone else's problem.

Today's breakfast consisted of jambalaya, buttermilk cornbread, creamed corn, and sweet tea, though coffee was still available for the purists. Since she'd already made everything yesterday, if she hurried things along, she could be out of there in thirty minutes tops—which was well before Shelley even thought about getting up.

"And don't forget I need your opinions on breakfast," she reminded them. "This is one of the recipes I plan to serve while the guests are here."

"Morning," Shelley called out. She dragged herself into the room looking like a character from a horror movie. Her long dark hair hung in limp, loose strands, concealing her face as she trudged forward. When she reached them, she plopped down next to Emilio, then face-planted on the table. "Coffee," she moaned. "I. Need. Coffee."

Since there was no use in telling her to get it herself, Grace went to the kitchen and poured her a coffee, placing the cup in front of her along with a bowl of jambalaya.

"I must admit, I didn't expect to see you this early," Grace said, more than a little annoyed to have her plan foiled once again.

Shelley lifted her head. "Shhh," then placed it back down on the table.

Choosing to ignore her, Grace turned to Molly. "Have all the rooms been booked?"

"Mm-hmm," Molly nodded, a Cheshire grin spreading across her face. "And I have a little surprise for you!"

Grace wasn't sure she could handle any more surprises. "Please don't tell me some of the guests are coming early. Or that you booked another 'influencer.'" She winced and turned toward Rebekah. "No offense," she said sheepishly.

"None taken," Rebekah replied, though her tone suggested otherwise.

"Carl and Katherine are coming!" Molly announced excitedly. "They reached out when they saw my post for the Mardi Gras event and told me they just had to come. They were a little hurt we didn't invite them first," Molly warned. "After all, as people who live in New Orleans, they are resident experts, so we need to make sure we make them feel extra welcome when they get here."

Emilio looked up from his phone, his brow furrowed. "Weren't they just here a few weeks ago for Grace's wedding?"

Grant patted him on the back. "When you're retired, you can travel as much as you want," he teased.

"I can't wait for those days!" he said dreamily.

"Take it from us," Granny said, pointing between her and Gladys, "don't wait. If you want to do something, find a way to do it while you're young. If you wait till you're our age, it might be too late."

Gladys elbowed Granny. "Hush, you. If this is about the Wheel, it is not too late. We are making that audition tape, and that is final!"

"Audition tape?" Shelley's head popped up, all traces of sleepiness disappearing as excitement took its place. "What kind of audition tape?"

Granny rolled her eyes. "Do not get her started," she groaned.

"Our favorite game show of all time is bringing back a special episode of couples week," Gladys explained. "It can be any type of couple: spouses, family/friends, even parent/child. I told Josie we need to send in our audition tape pronto! Wouldn't it be crazy if we were chosen?"

"It would be crazy, all right," Granny snarked. "We're older than dirt, Gladys. There's no way they're going to choose us out of the thousands of entries they're sure to receive."

Gladys clucked her tongue. "When did you become so negative?"

Granny opened her mouth to reply, but Gladys waved her off.

"Anyway, even if they don't pick us, I still think it would be a hoot to film a tape—even if *some of us* are being fuddy-duddies about it."

"I could help you," Shelley offered.

All eyes turned toward her.

"What?" she asked, taken aback by the sudden attention. "I *am* an expert on filming videos. Why, I bet I know enough tips and tricks that, with my coaching, you'll be practically guaranteed a spot on the show!"

This would keep Shelley out of trouble, Grace silently mused. Or it would get Granny and Gladys into trouble. Was it worth the risk? She decided it was.

"I think that sounds like a great idea!" Grace said enthusiastically. "You two have always loved that show, and I know you will regret it if you don't at least try."

"See!" Gladys said to Granny. "Even Grace supports us. You have no reason to say no now."

Granny still looked unsure, but she eventually nodded. "Alright, let's do it."

"Yay!" Shelley said, clapping enthusiastically. "You two will not regret this!" She reached for her coffee, her nose wrinkling when she saw the bowl of jambalaya. "What's this?"

"A new recipe I'm working on," Grace explained. "Try it, you might like it."

Shelley shook her head. "I am *not* eating *that* for breakfast. I'll take eggs sunny-side up, toast—but I want it cut diagonally, not vertically—bacon, and a side of hash browns. You know where to find me, but if we're in the middle of a scene, feel free to set it off to the side."

The three of them rose from the table, Shelley looping one of her arms through one of theirs. "Oh, and Grace," Shelley called over her shoulder, "make sure you stay out of the camera frame. We wouldn't want to 'accidentally film you without your permission.'" She smiled sweetly, then walked off to Granny's room, chatting excitedly.

"You know you're going to regret that," Rebekah said once they were out of earshot.

"I have no doubt," Grace replied. "But at least they'll be occupied for a while." She turned her attention back to Molly. "Now, where were we?"

Molly blinked a few times, then looked down at her notebook. "Ah yes, Carl and Katherine will arrive on Friday to help make sure things are 'authentic.' The rest of the guests will arrive Monday."

So guests were coming early. Oh well, at least it was Carl and Katherine. Grace loved it when they were here, so this was a good thing. "What about the others?" she asked, curious as to who she'd be sharing her home with. Or was that former home? Grace pushed those thoughts aside. No more of that nonsense—this place would always be home, even if she lived somewhere else.

"Let's see," Molly said, consulting her list again. "We have Jasmine and Dwayne, a couple from Overland Park, KS; Eva and Phillip, a couple from Joplin; and then there's—" she hesitated for a moment, an indiscernible look crossing her face. "Then there's Jack, a man from New York."

Rebekah looked up from her phone at the mention of her old state. "Where in New York?"

Molly cleared her throat. "Manhattan. Which is a really big city, so I doubt you know him or anything."

"Okayyy," Rebekah drawled, her brows furrowed as she stared at Molly. "That was a really weird thing to say."

"Well, you know, I just didn't want you to worry after that inci— never mind," Molly stammered. She gathered her things, then grabbed the baby carrier. "I'm sorry, guys, there's just a lot going on at work, and I'm really distracted. The important thing to know is that the rooms are fully booked and everything is great." She gave them a quick wave, then left, Grant and Emilio following.

Grace and Rebekah exchanged looks.

"Was it me, or did she seem nervous?" Rebekah asked.

"It was not you," Grace replied, a little stunned to see her unflappable friend flapped. Was that a word? What was the opposite of unflappable? She would have to remember to look that up later. "Anyway, where are we with the carnival?"

It was Rebekah's turn to consult her notes, though she had to pull out her laptop to do so. "They will be here Thursday and plan to be up and running by Friday night."

"Isn't that a little early?" Grace asked, surprised they weren't starting on Tuesday like they had planned.

Rebekah made a face. "This was the best I could do on short notice," she explained.

"What does that mean?" Grace asked, her concern growing by the minute. Her guests would be there for nine days, and she most definitely did not have nine activities to keep them busy. She was counting on the carnival to entertain them. Without that, she was hosed.

"It means they'll be here from Friday to Thursday," Rebekah informed her. "They were going to stay until the following Friday, but we need them packed up and out of the way for the parade on Saturday, so they have to leave a day early."

"I think you mean five days early," Grace grumbled. What was she supposed to do now? Okay, most of the activities she had planned would take place during those five days, and yes, the carnival would only hold its charm for so long, but she still hated to think she was losing a source of entertainment. "I guess I'll just have to come up with something else," she said out loud.

Rebekah looked up. "We don't have time for something else," she reminded her.

"Did I say that out loud?" Grace asked, the answer obvious.

"Yes, you did, smartypants," Rebekah said. "But, Grace, I'm serious. We already have too much going on. We simply don't have the time or manpower to add another thing at this stage of the game. Your guests are adults; they can always drive up to the city and go to the movies or something if they get bored."

"They can do that anywhere," Grace whined. "The whole point of these experiences is that we offer something they can't do at home!"

Shelley ran through the room, a big smile on her face. "Hey guys!" she yelled as she passed them. She returned a few minutes later with a camera, a tripod, and some other equipment balanced in her one good arm. "Bye guys!" she called out as she ran back to Granny's room.

"I'm really going to regret this, aren't I?" Grace asked Rebekah.

"Nah, I'm sure it's harmless fun," Rebekah assured her. "Shelley did leave her skateboard at the hotel, right?"

An image of Shelley, Granny, and Gladys riding a skateboard down the stairs flashed before Grace's eyes, but she quickly shook it off. "Actually, I didn't see a skateboard when I was there. She must have left it somewhere."

"I'll look for it next time I'm there," Rebekah offered. "For all we know, she left it on the stairs, and someone's going to end up on the ride of their life!"

Grace winced at the notion, then narrowed her eyes. "Wait a minute, what do you mean next time you're there? Aren't you staying there?"

Rebekah looked away, her cheeks reddening. "Don't hate me, but…"

"But what?" Grace asked, her earlier concern returning.

"But it's kind of scary staying there alone," Rebekah admitted. "There's all kinds of noises—that I'm sure have rational explanations—but it's not always easy to remind yourself of that when it's dark out, you know?"

Oh yeah, she knew. Grace had spent many late nights there alone when she was getting the hotel ready for Evie's family last July. She'd experienced those noises firsthand, and while she wasn't someone who believed in ghosts, it didn't take much for her overactive imagination to run wild with possibilities. "So where did you go?" Grace asked. "My offer still stands if you want my room."

"I appreciate that, but Thorne has agreed to let me stay with him. I know people will wag their tongues at us shacking up before we're married," she continued, "but it's only temporary."

"If you're worried about that, you can always stay at the farm with me and Cole," Grace offered. "The guest room is all yours if you want it."

Rebekah snorted. "I will not be a third wheel to a newlywed couple," she said with a laugh. "But I do appreciate the offer." She closed her laptop and put it back in her bag.

"The Mayor's Masquerade Ball really does have a nice ring to it, don't you think?" Grace asked dreamily. "I mean, I know it's not the Governor's Ball, but it's still more classy than just a ball at the community center."

"That reminds me," Rebekah said, snapping her fingers. "There is the ballroom at the hotel. We could have the ball there instead of the community center if you think it's big enough?"

Grace tried to picture the ballroom in her head. It wasn't a room she went in often; in fact, she'd only been in there once when they first toured the hotel. "I need to go see what kind of condition it's in, and then check with Grant and Molly. But if they're on board, I think that would be awesome!"

Rebekah nodded. "Let me know ASAP, okay? And by the way, the jambalaya needs a little extra spice."

Shelley ran through a second time. "Hey guys!" She continued through the door, then returned a minute later, Lyda in tow. "Bye guys!" she called out, a director's beret now on her head.

Lyda waved as she followed Shelley, an identical beret covering her pixie-style hairdo.

"Do you think..." Grace trailed off, pointing toward Granny's room.

"Nope," Rebekah said, shaking her head. "Let them have their fun."

It was tempting to argue, but Grace ultimately agreed. She was a little jealous she wasn't included, but figured it was probably better that way. The less she knew, the less she would fret—and not fretting was always a good thing.

-Thirteen-

Grace woke up to the smell of... bacon? She sat up in bed, just in time to see her husband walk through the door, breakfast tray in hand.

"Good morning, beautiful," he said, setting the tray over her lap, then kissing her forehead. "Happy Valentine's Day!"

She looked down at the tray, her eyes widening as she took in the heart-shaped pancakes, perfectly crisped bacon, coffee, orange juice, and a single red rose in a crystal vase. "You did this for me?" she asked, her eyes tearing as she looked up at him in awe.

"Of course I did, silly," he said, climbing into bed beside her and wrapping his arms around her shoulders. "It's our first Valentine's Day together as husband and wife. I have to make it special."

"I had no idea I was marrying the world's most romantic man," she said dreamily. "Though I guess I should have figured that out when he sent a horse-drawn carriage to take me to our wedding!" She fed him a bite of pancakes, then took one herself, moaning in pleasure at how light and fluffy they were. "If I'd known you knew how to cook like this, you'd have been the one doing all the cooking this past year," she teased.

Cole chuckled. "I still have a few surprises up my sleeve," he said as he kissed his way down her neck. He stopped when he reached her shoulder, then carefully got out of bed. "If you can manage to be home in time for dinner, you might just get another one." He winked at her, then left the room, whistling as he prepared to leave to do the morning chores.

Who was this man, and what did he do with her husband?! Cole had always been attentive—and she had no complaints in the romance department—but this was a whole new level from him, and she was here for it! The only question she had now was, what could she do for him in return?

Sure, she already had a gift picked out for him, but, she hated to admit, it was a bottle of his favorite cologne, which was so uninspiring it paled in comparison to the breakfast he'd served alone. If he had more planned, that made things worse!

"Ugh!" she yelled in frustration. Men have it so easy. All they have to do is go to the store, and they'll find a plethora of options: flowers, candy, jewelry, stuffed animals, all geared toward women. *Cole didn't give you any of those*, a voice in her head whispered. "Fine, so he's better in that regard too!"

"Maybe I should stop talking to myself," she muttered. There was still plenty of time to figure things out. First, she would finish her breakfast—no sense in letting this delicious food go to waste. Then she would call an emergency meeting with all her friends. Surely one of them would have an idea. If they didn't, well, she would cross that bridge when she came to it!

***

"What's the emergency?" Molly asked as she entered the dining room.

Rebekah, Lyda, Granny, Gladys, and, for reasons known only to her, Shelley was already there, waiting on Grace to reveal the reason she'd summoned them. She would have loved it if Evie, Cassie, and Vanessa could have come, but since they couldn't get away from work, Grace had to hope they could find a solution without them.

"As you know, today is Valentine's Day," Grace began. She watched their faces for signs of the same uncertainty she was facing, but there were none. "I need help coming up with a gift for Cole," she pleaded.

Molly blinked in surprise. "This is your definition of an emergency?"

"Don't start with me," Grace said sullenly. "I once ran five blocks in the heat because you made me think you were having a pregnancy emergency."

The others looked at her, curious expressions on their faces.

"She wasn't, by the way," Grace pouted. "Anyway, Cole surprised me with breakfast in bed this morning, and all I got him was a stupid bottle of cologne. You have to help me come up with something better."

"It's not supposed to be a competition," Lyda pointed out.

Grace shook her head. "You don't understand. Cole already gets up at five-thirty each morning to do chores, which means he sacrificed a half hour of much-needed sleep to do something for me. I want to show him he means just as much to me as I do to him." She looked helplessly at the other women. Why were none of them offering solutions?

"Don't look at me," Lyda replied. "I'm divorced, and even when I was married, my husband was never around for these kinds of things."

Granny and Gladys exchanged glances.

"We got the guys the new Clive Cussler book, but that doesn't sound like something you would get Cole," Granny said apologetically.

"I got Grant tickets to one of the Kansas City Royals spring training games, but that doesn't sound like something Cole would want either," Molly said.

Her hope fading fast, Grace turned to Rebekah. "Please tell me you have an idea?"

Rebekah shook her head. "I'm sorry, Grace, but Thorne and I agreed on takeout and a movie. We're simply too busy for anything else."

Grace sighed and put her face in her hands. What was she supposed to do now? She was running out of time if she planned to be home by dinner, and she really wanted to be home for dinner.

"Well?" Shelley said, glancing up from the fingernails she was filing.

"Well what?" Grace asked.

"Aren't you going to ask me?"

Why on earth would Shelley of all people think Grace wanted advice from her? The woman who cheated with her sister's fiancé for years. The woman who then cheated on him with another man. The woman who—well, you get the point. Then again, she was desperate...

"Okay, Shelley, do you have any suggestions?" Grace asked sweetly.

Shelley put down the nail file and sat up straight. "Yes, I do. Thank you for asking. You claim that your store-bought gift is inadequate compared to the thoughtful homemade one Cole gave you, correct?"

Grace nodded.

"So why don't you make him a gift? Bake him his favorite dessert, give him coupons for a back massage—you know, things like that?" She gave Grace one of her looks that screamed duh, then went back to filing her nails.

That was actually a really great idea. In fact, she still had time to do both of those if she hurried. "Thank you, Shelley, you're a lifesaver!" Grace called over her shoulder as she raced out of the house and to her car.

Who would have thought something good would come out of Shelley staying with them?

***

The chocolate torte was just about ready to come out of the oven when Cole walked in the door.

"Something smells good," he said, kissing her neck. "Something looks good too," he said, twirling her around, then wrapping his arms around her waist.

Grace giggled, her arms instinctively reaching up toward his neck. She pulled his head down to hers and kissed him, reluctantly pulling apart when the timer on the oven went off. "Why don't you go get cleaned up while I finish in here," she suggested.

"Okay, but I'm pretty sure I'm the one who's supposed to cook for you," he reminded her.

Despite Shelley's suggestions, Grace had struggled to figure out what to do. Making Cole's favorite dessert had been easy, putting together his gift bag full of coupons and cologne had been even easier, but then she'd run into the problem of dinner. Sure, he said he planned to cook for her, and she didn't want to take that away from him, but she didn't want to waste precious time waiting on the London broil to cook either. In the end, she'd decided to go for it and make the food herself. Hopefully, he wouldn't be too upset when he came back and saw the surprise she had set up for him.

By the time he came back—freshly showered and shaved—the candles were lit, soft jazz music played in the background, the fire crackled in the fireplace, and dinner was served on their little table for two.

Cole took it all in, a hint of disappointment in his eyes. "Looks like we had the same idea," he finally said.

"You spoiled me this morning," she replied, wrapping her arms around his neck. "It was my turn to spoil you." She kissed him until his disappointment melted away, then led him over to the table.

Several minutes passed as they filled their plates, Grace anxiously waiting for the appropriate time to give him the rest of his gift.

"How was your day?" she asked between bites. "Anything eventful happen?"

He finished chewing, then gave her a thoughtful look. "Not really. How about you?"

Grace narrowed her eyes. "What aren't you telling me?"

Cole shook his head. "Not tonight, baby," he said firmly. "I am not wasting my night with you on things that can wait until the morning."

She wanted to argue but knew it was pointless. If Cole thought it was best to leave it till the morning, nothing short of begging would change his mind. And honestly, did she really want to spoil their evening? Especially when she'd gone to so much trouble, dressing up for him in her favorite red dress, baking his favorite dessert...

With that decided, she reached down beside her chair and grabbed the gift bag she'd made for him, then handed it to him.

"What, no argument?" he teased, reaching over to feel her forehead with the back of his hand. "You're not getting sick on me, are you?"

"You're lucky you're so handsome," she laughed, pushing his hand away. "Now open your present before I take it back!"

He pulled the gift paper out of the bag and set it off to the side, then pulled the first item out of the bag: gift certificates. "What are these?" he asked as he studied the paper. "Good for one massage..."

"I thought you might appreciate those after a long day out in the field," Grace explained.

"It's a pretty big stack," he said as he fanned it open. "You're going to be awfully busy this summer!" he teased. Cole leaned over and kissed her cheek, then pulled the next present out of the bag. "Aww, my favorite cologne. Thank you!"

He surprised her by getting out of his seat and disappearing to the back room. She was about to follow him and ask if she'd offended him when he returned with a long, black velvet box and slid it over in front of her.

"Happy Valentine's Day," he said, kissing her cheek.

She opened the box and found a gold chain bracelet nestled against the padded insert. In the middle of the chain was a gold heart with their initials intertwined. "It's beautiful," she gasped, pulling it out of the box so she could clasp it around her wrist.

Cole reached over to help, then moved the insert to reveal several more gold hearts. "If you ever decide you want kids, we can put their initials on the extra hearts and add them to your bracelet," he explained. He brought her hand to his lips and kissed it gently. "No pressure, though."

Her heart squeezed at the thought, the idea of holding his baby in her arms no longer so scary. As the candlelight glinted off the metal heart, a vision of more hearts dangling with theirs nearly brought tears to her eyes. So when he scooped her up into his arms and carried her back to their bedroom, she let him.

-Twelve-

I t was still dark out when Grace opened her eyes. She glanced at the alarm clock on the nightstand and saw it was five forty-five. Somehow, she'd managed to sleep through the alarm. A curious thing, given that had never happened before. She rolled over just in time to see Cole tiptoeing out of the room.

"What are you doing?" she called out, startling him so badly he dropped the pair of socks he was holding.

"I was trying to leave without waking you up," he said as he bent down to retrieve the garment. "I figured you could use the extra sleep."

Even though she was certain it was too dark for him to see her face, she narrowed her eyes at him and scowled. "You mean you were trying to leave without telling me whatever it is you said could wait till now," she accused.

Cole walked over to the bed and sat down next to her. "Contrary to popular opinion, I do not enjoy keeping things from you," he drawled. He leaned down and kissed her shoulder. "You were sleeping so peacefully I honestly didn't have the heart to wake you."

Well, now didn't she feel like a jerk. "I'm sorry," she whispered, her arms reaching out for him. "I might be a tad paranoid."

"Just a tad," he teased, holding his thumb and pointer finger together. "The question is why?"

Grace shrugged. "Same reason as always, I guess. I'm worried that Riley will leave and you'll be back to doing everything by yourself. And then there goes our time together."

"If Riley were to leave—and that's a big if—we would just hire someone else, okay? There's no need to panic and assume the worst."

She knew he was right, but if it was that easy to find a farmhand, why did it take him so long to do it in the first place? A question for another day. "So then what is going on?"

Cole nudged her over, then slid under the covers and snuggled up against her, her back to his chest. "I asked Riley if he had plans for last night, and he got real quiet and said no. When I tried to probe further, he shut down and made up an excuse to run off. This is pure speculation, but it seems possible he and Katie have either broken up or are on the verge of it."

Gladys's words about someone stealing from the town rushed into her head and out of her mouth before she could think better of it. "Gladys said she overheard someone may have been stealing money from the town," Grace blurted out. "What if it's Katie?"

"Sounds to me like unfounded gossip," Cole replied. "If this is a rumor going around, imagine how Katie feels right now."

Grace hadn't thought about that. "Gladys never mentioned her by name, so I don't think anyone is talking about her specifically. I do know she hasn't been at the meetings, but I suppose there are other explanations for that."

He sighed, then rolled her over to face him. "I think it's best we stay out of this, okay? If something is going on, as a member of the town council, you'll find out soon enough. If there's not, you don't want to add fuel to the fire."

"Of course I don't," Grace said, hurt that he'd think such a thing about her. "All I wanted was to make sure Riley has every reason to stay put. I have zero desire to implicate his girlfriend in some kind of heist." She looked down so he couldn't see the hurt in her eyes, then back up at him when he lifted her chin, her eyes flashing in annoyance.

"I wasn't accusing you," he said gently. "I just know how easily these things can get out of hand."

She wanted to stay mad at him, but it was hard when he made sense like that. Harder still when he began to trace soothing circles on her back. "We just had a fight..."

Cole chuckled, his lips against her ear. "Guess that means we have some making up to do."

***

Grace had wanted to meet everyone for breakfast, but had to go to the hotel instead. The carnival crew was expected around ten, and she'd somehow forgotten to make sure the rooms were ready to go. Now that Jilly was busy at the bakery and no longer able to help, Grace had a feeling things were about to get crazy. Maybe she should have spent some time looking for a replacement instead of whatever it was she'd been doing this last week. She honestly couldn't remember anymore; time seemed to pass by in a blur these days.

She pulled the cleaning cart out of the closet and wheeled it to the first room. Thankfully, the rooms were still clean from the last time guests had checked out, so they only needed clean sheets and towels, a light dusting, and vacuuming. Easy peasy—until she realized she needed to do this twenty more times.

As she wandered between the rooms, fluffing pillows and ensuring all the televisions still had working remotes, she tried to think of someone she could hire. Lyda had filled in for Jilly over New Year's, but between her kids, her business, and her booth at the carnival, she would be too busy. Grace supposed she could offer the job to one of the seniors at the high school, but again, the teen would be at school during the hours Grace would need them most. Who did that leave? Anybody? She would have to ask Molly to post about it on the town's social media page and see if anyone was interested.

When she was convinced the rooms were ready for guests, she checked the time and discovered she had an hour to kill before the workers arrived. Which was nowhere near enough time for a bulk food run, but too much time to hang around twiddling her thumbs. Since she hadn't checked on Jilly in a while, she decided to walk to the bakery and see how her friend was getting along now that Bea had taken off for parts unknown.

Ding Ding

"Be right with you!" Jilly called out from the kitchen.

Grace walked over to the display cases and eyed the brightly colored macarons. What was it she'd read about special food during Mardi Gras? She opened up the saved tabs on her phone's browser and did a quick search for the one on desserts. "Oh my gosh," her hand flew to her mouth.

"What?" Jilly asked as she rounded the corner. "What's wrong?"

Her eyes widened in horror. "I forgot to talk to you about the king cakes!" Grace croaked out. She slapped a palm to her forehead. "How could I forget one of the most important parts of Mardi Gras?"

Jilly whipped her phone out of her back pocket and typed a few words. "Oh yeah, the colorful cakes with the plastic babies. How many do you need?"

How many did she need? At least five for the B&B, though depending on the size, ten might be a safer number. Her plan had been to have one for each room as a welcome gift and then have some with different flavors to serve as dessert. She counted that out on her fingers. Definitely ten. "I need at least ten for the B&B, but Jilly, there's going to be tons of people in town over the next week and a half, and I wouldn't be surprised if every one of them wanted a cake!"

It was Jilly's turn for her eyes to widen. "I can't handle that," she stammered. "Jenny still hates me, and I haven't been able to find anyone to take her place. I'm barely hanging on as it is!"

"I was going to ask Molly to place a job posting for me, but maybe we should have her place one for you, too. Even if you only get a part-time helper after school, that would still be better than nothing."

Jilly didn't look convinced. "Even if I hired a small army, I still wouldn't be able to handle that many orders in such a short amount of time," she protested. "I've never made a king cake before, so I'd need time to perfect a recipe. Not to mention I'd have to order supplies..." she trailed off. "Maybe I could offer Mardi Gras-themed donuts?" she asked hopefully.

Grace felt awful; this was all her fault. "How about this? I need to make a food run anyway, so you send a list of things you need and I'll get them while I'm out. We'll have Molly place the wanted ad, but in the meantime, I'll help as much as I'm able. We'll agree to do donuts, since those are easier, but in between batches we'll practice making king cakes. Deal?"

"I think I can work with that," Jilly replied, her eyes narrowed as she tried to do the numbers in her head. "But Grace, how will we know what a king cake is supposed to taste like?"

"I'll hit up a few bakeries in the city and see if they have any," Grace replied. This trip was becoming too big for one person to handle on their own, but she had no intention of telling Jilly that. She would have to borrow Cole's truck and see if Rebekah was free. "Text me the list ASAP, and I'll let you know when I'm on my way back."

Grace checked her watch again; there was just enough time to talk to Molly and still get back to the hotel before people began to arrive. She waved goodbye, then quickly made her way over to the office, pausing to say hello to Tess when she saw her standing by the coffee maker in the lobby. "You look rough," Grace blurted out. "I'm so sorry, I didn't mean it like that."

Tess looked up from the coffee she'd been watching drip slowly into her cup. "It's okay, I know what you mean. It's nice to see you again, Grace."

"It's nice to see you, too," Grace replied, unsure of where to go from there. She did not have time for a proper conversation but didn't want to leave things where they were after her giant faux pas. "Is there anything I can do to help?"

She shook her head. "I appreciate the offer, but I think Austin and I finally have things under control. I just need a few days to catch up on sleep. Or maybe weeks." She nodded to herself. "Definitely weeks." Her coffee cup now full, she wandered off toward her office, pausing in the doorway to give Grace a small wave.

Another glance at her watch showed it was time to hustle, so she hurried down the hall to Molly's office and dropped into a chair in front of her desk.

Molly raised a brow, then looked pointedly at the clock. "To what do I owe this unexpected visit?" she asked. "Shouldn't you be at the hotel?"

"Yeah, yeah," Grace waved her off. She made quick work of telling Molly what she wanted, then stood to leave. "How soon can you get it done?" she asked.

"I can make the post now, but I have no idea how long it will take for someone to respond, nor can I guarantee the ones that do will be serious. Plus, we'll need time to do background checks and get them set up on payroll."

Grace took a calming breath. "Please do your best to speed things along. Jilly is drowning, and it won't be long before I'm joining her if we don't get some help around here fast."

"I'll do what I can," Molly promised. "But we need to prepare ourselves to have to wing it this time. If that means I need to help out at the hotel or the B&B, then so be it."

The last time Molly had offered to help at the B&B was the first Christmas she'd come to stay here. Ever since then, she'd been too busy running her marketing agency to have time to think to help. Something was definitely going on, and the more she thought of it, the more determined she became to get to the bottom of it.

Since she really did need to get back, for now she nodded and headed for the door. "Hey," she said, pausing just outside. "Where was Katie yesterday? I haven't seen her in a while, and I need to check in with her on some of the arrangements for the upcoming events."

That was only a partial lie. She didn't actually have to check in, but she did like to keep Katie informed in case people called town hall with questions.

"Katie has taken an extended leave from her job as the town manager," Molly said slowly. "Rebekah is acting as the liaison between the B&B, the town, and the volunteer committees, so if there's something you need to discuss, she's the one to do it with."

"I don't suppose you're going to provide any more details than that?"

Molly shook her head. "That is all I'm at liberty to say at this time." She looked at her computer screen. "Now it's time for you to run—literally. People will be arriving any minute, and we don't want them showing up to an empty hotel."

"Yes, ma'am," she gave a mock salute, then took off running as suggested.

When she reached the hotel, the first car was just pulling up, giving Grace mere minutes to get the computer booted up and running before the chaos of checking people in began. It was hard to focus on the task at hand, her mind replaying the part about Katie taking a leave of absence over and over. Was she sick? That would explain why Riley was upset. Had they broken up and she left town to avoid him?

It seemed impossible Katie could have been the one caught stealing. She'd been the town manager for years, and as far as Grace could tell, was well liked by everyone. If she were in trouble, Grace had no doubt the entire town would pitch in to help her. So if it wasn't her, then what was going on? More importantly, how much did Rebekah know?

-Eleven-

"How did the check-ins go yesterday?" Molly asked as she entered the kitchen. "Did you make it back in time?"

Grace looked up from the baked goods she was assembling on a platter. So far she'd been up since four, worked three hours at the bakery, set up a breakfast buffet at the hotel, and had just enough time to drop off donuts and muffins at the house before she had to be at the check-in meeting at Addie's. Simply put, she was tired, wired on coffee, and in no mood to discuss whether or not she was handling her business—which she was, thank you very much.

"Did you post the ads?" Grace asked instead. Finding help was the only thing she cared about, and if Molly didn't come through soon, Grace was going to take her up on her offer to help out. Especially since she still had to get the rooms ready for her guests—starting with the one for Carl and Katherine—who were expected that afternoon.

She bristled a bit at Grace's abrupt change of topic, but she appeared to think better of mentioning it. "I did," she confirmed. "We've received plenty of comments, but no one has expressed interest as of yet. It's been less than twenty-four hours, so that's not exactly a surprise."

While that was probably true, Grace still didn't like it. "Are you going to the meeting?"

"Is there a separate conversation going on in your head?" Molly asked. "You're giving me whiplash with these abrupt changes of topic."

"Sorry," Grace muttered. She set the platter on the breakfast bar, then washed her hands. "There's a lot going on, and I feel pressed for time." She put her coat on and grabbed her keys. "Are you coming or not?"

Molly grabbed a donut off the platter, then rushed after Grace. "What has gotten into you this morning?"

They were seated in the car and on their way to Addie's before Grace replied. "I think I've become lazy," Grace mused. "For an entire year, it was go, go, go—and while I didn't love the constant pressure, I got used to it, you know? But then I had all that time off for the wedding, and then the honeymoon, and now I'm struggling to get back into the groove."

"That doesn't make you lazy, silly," Molly said, rolling her eyes. "It just makes you human. I felt the same way after I took time off when I had Eliza."

Grace remembered Molly struggling to take time off; she did not remember her struggling to adjust when she went back to work. Then again, she did hire Tess, so maybe Grace had been too busy to see the struggle. "Any tips on how to get back into the swing of things?" She pulled into the parking lot and turned to face Molly.

Molly considered her for a moment. "I wish I had something to say that didn't sound trite or cliché, but unfortunately I don't." She reached over and clasped Grace's hand. "We will get through this," she said, squeezing her hand tight. "And next time we'll plan things out farther in advance so we won't feel as rushed, okay?"

"That would help," Grace said softly. It was time to toughen up and 'lock in,' as the kids say. "Let's do this!"

Addie's was a little less crowded this time, but not by much. As Grace walked to the back, she searched the crowd for Granny and Gladys, then waved when she saw them in what she assumed was their usual spot.

When it was her time to speak, an idea formed as she looked at the dozens of people before her. "Good morning!" she said to the crowd. "I would like to start by thanking you again for your support. The sign-up sheets are full, and Main Street is already coming together! If we work hard today, it should be ready by the time the carnival opens tonight!"

The crowd clapped and cheered, their enthusiasm palpable.

Mayor Allen clinked his glass to get their attention.

Grace smiled at him in thanks, then turned back to the volunteers. "There are a couple of opportunities I would like to tell you about before we leave today." She took a deep breath to calm the anxiety that was currently rearing its ugly head. "If any of you are interested, Jilly is hiring over at the bakery, and I am looking for help at the B&B." She looked over their faces, hopeful at least a few of them would show signs they were indeed interested.

A woman in front raised her hand. "I've been looking for a part-time job, and would be happy to help out at the B&B, but I'm only available from eight to three while my kiddos are in school. Would that work?"

"That's exactly what I need," Grace said, her voice coming out in a whoosh. "Talk to me after the meeting and I'll get your information."

One down, one to go. Was her plan really going to work? She scanned the group a second time, but no one else raised their hand. Were they still mad about the Jenny thing? Or did they really just not want to work at a bakery? Grace wouldn't blame them if that were the case. She didn't love it either, but if she couldn't find someone, that meant she was stuck with the job.

Her anxiety began to morph into desperation as the silence became awkward.

"We'll do it," Granny said, she and Gladys raising their hands and waving them toward Grace.

Grace's eyes widened in surprise. Was Granny serious? Surely not. She and Gladys were in their eighties, for pete's sake, not to mention their health problems. How on earth did they think working a demanding job in a bakery was a good idea? "Um, okay," Grace stammered. "Thank you, I'll talk to you after the meeting as well."

With nothing left to say, she turned the floor over to Mayor Allen and returned to Molly's side. "Can you believe that?" she whispered.

"We need to talk to Jenny asap," Molly whispered back. "This little feud has gone on long enough."

Since Jenny was working for Addie, Grace was a little apprehensive about approaching her. Attempting to poach one of Addie's waitresses might not go over so well, especially at a time like this. But did she have a choice?

"I'll talk to Jenny if you'll get that woman's information," Grace offered.

"Deal."

As they waited for the room to clear, Grace anxiously tapped her foot. When enough people had left, she marched over to the counter and waved Jenny over.

"What can I get you?" Jenny asked, a bored expression on her face.

Grace didn't have time to waste, so she decided to cut straight to the point. "What would it take to get you to go back to the bakery?"

Jenny's head whipped back, her eyes blinking in surprise. "Hmmph, I gave it six months before Jilly failed, yet you're telling me it took less than two?" She snorted in derision.

"Well? What would it take? It doesn't have to be permanent, just long enough to help us get through the next week and a half."

"Why would I do that?" Jenny snapped. "Did you forget why I quit in the first place?"

This was going to be harder than she thought, though why she ever thought it would be easy was beyond her. "I have not forgotten," Grace said, her tone even. "Nor am I asking you to forget. This isn't about Bea, Jilly, or even the bakery. It's about the town. We need you, Jenny. You are the only one with enough experience to be of any actual help."

"I don't know," Jenny replied, her earlier display of hostility lessening. "I really feel like you're asking a lot of me. How am I supposed to get along with that bakery-stealing woman for twelve hours a day?"

The urge to defend Jilly was strong, but Grace held her tongue. They could argue till the cows came home over whether or not Jilly actually stole anything, especially since it was never Jenny's to begin with. But now was not the time.

"Headphones," Grace said bluntly. "I'm going to be there too, so each morning we will assign tasks. Then you put your headphones in, do your part, and at the end of the day, we'll all go our separate ways—only you'll be seen as a hero."

"A hero, eh? I like the sound of that," Jenny said, nodding along as she thought about Grace's offer. "Fine, I'm in."

Had Grace heard her correctly? Did she really just agree? Was she about to step outside and see pigs flying? "That's great!" Grace said enthusiastically. "I will see you tomorrow morning at four thirty!"

Now all she had to do was break the news to Jilly, and Grace wasn't so sure she was going to be as thrilled. Oh well, that would also have to be a problem for later.

***

"Actually, there is a Mardi Gras Queen," Carl informed Grace. "And a King. The tradition goes back to at least the forties."

Shelley stuck her tongue out at Grace. "See, I told you so!"

"Okay, fine, I was wrong," Grace admitted. "Do we have to have one, though?" she asked Carl.

Carl and Katherine exchanged a look.

"You don't have to do anything," Carl replied. "But if you want to stick to tradition…"

Grace sighed. Did she want to stick to tradition? She highly doubted anyone would complain if she skipped this particular part. Then again, she also doubted Shelley would let it go, especially now that Carl had told her she was right. "How do we go about choosing the King and Queen?" Grace asked.

"I feel like I need to give you a history lesson to properly explain this," Carl told her. "New Orleans has what we call Krewes. These are private social clubs that are responsible for the planning and execution of parades, floats, balls, costumes, and everything else associated with Mardi Gras. Each one has their own King and Queen, and how they choose them varies by the club," Carl explained.

It wasn't easy, but Grace tried to read between the lines. "I'm guessing money plays a role?"

Carl nodded. "Wealth, social status, sometimes celebrity status. It just depends on the Krewe, how long they've existed, and what kind of traditions they've established over the years."

An interesting thought occurred to Grace. "Have either of you ever been a King or Queen?"

He laughed, the sound harsh. "I was ex-communicated long before I might have been considered for such a prestigious honor."

Grace winced. "I'm so sorry, I shouldn't have asked. That was highly insensitive of me."

His face softened. "It's okay," he said, pulling her in for a side hug. "I thought I had finally let go of all my resentment. I guess I still have some work to do on that front."

"I don't believe it would have mattered either way," Katherine replied. "Our family had money, but lacked the social standing." She shrugged. "Regardless, it's up to you if you have one or not. But if you want to, I suggest keeping things simple and holding a vote. Let the town decide who they want to represent them."

One more thing to deal with, but okay, Grace could handle this. Or rather, Rebekah could handle it. This was more up her alley anyway.

"I'm off to campaign!" Shelley announced. She narrowed her eyes at Grace. "Don't even think about running against me. I was homecoming queen three years in a row, and I'm not afraid to fight dirty if I have to!"

Grace watched her go, then turned back to the others. "That woman is going to be the death of me."

Katherine chuckled. "She seems nice, just a bit... overzealous."

"Let's see if you still feel that way in a couple of days," Grace replied. She went to the kitchen and grabbed the plate of beignets, a square of fried dough, typically eaten hot—though hers were now cold—and sprinkled with confectioners sugar, she'd made that morning, then brought them back to the table for Carl and Katherine to try. "Be honest," she told them. "If anyone will know if these taste right, it's you two."

She watched them intently as they each tried one, looking for signs they either liked or hated them. Maybe she should have given more thought to her menu choices before she decided on this theme. Who was she to think she could master the art of French cuisine in a week?

Carl finished his beignet, then licked the sugar off his fingers. "It tastes a bit like a donut, but it's still really good. I doubt anyone would complain."

Katherine nodded. "I agree. It's not quite as light and airy as a traditional beignet, but I'd have no problem eating them."

That wasn't quite the reaction Grace had hoped for, but at this point, she would take it. "Thanks you guys, I appreciate your honesty." She checked her watch and saw it was almost time for the carnival to start. "There's just enough time for you guys to unpack before it's time to go. Want to meet me in the foyer in thirty minutes?"

They rose from their seats and prepared to go upstairs.

"Sounds good," Carl said. "Will we be seeing your other half tonight?"

"Cole should be here around the time we're ready to go!"

Once they'd left, she pulled out her phone and checked in with Rebekah to make sure everything was ready for that night. Somehow, she'd gotten so busy she'd failed to talk to Jilly about Jenny, which she really needed to do before tomorrow morning. She had also forgotten about the new woman who had said she wanted to work for Grace. There was just too much to do and not enough time to do it.

And whose fault is that? asked the annoying voice in her head.

"Mine," Grace answered with a sigh. "It's mine."

Days till Mardi Gras

-Ten-

Buzz Buzz Buzz

Grace opened one eye and glared at the clock, then quickly reached over to shut off the offending alarm before it woke up Cole. Why had she agreed to help Jilly at the bakery? And why had she stayed out so late the night before when she knew she would have to get up at four the next morning? Speaking of Jilly...

She popped out of bed in a panic; she forgot to warn Jilly that Jenny was coming to help! Out of all the things to forget, this had to be the worst. She simply *must* beat Jenny to the bakery—it was the only way to ensure peace.

"What are you doing?" Cole asked, his eyes still closed as he burrowed deeper under the covers.

"I'm getting ready to go to the bakery," Grace replied as she pulled on her jeans. She walked over to his side of the bed and bent down to kiss his forehead. "Go back to sleep," she whispered. "I'll see you later."

Grace gave one last forlorn look at her bed, then left the room. How had Bea done this for forty years? Especially during the winter months when it was still so cold and dark out? Better yet, how was Jilly doing it now? And with two little ones at home to boot? They must be morning people, something Grace discovered long ago she was not, despite all the early morning activities she always seemed to get roped into.

The time on the car's dashboard read four fifteen when Grace pulled into a parking spot behind the bakery. When she saw hers was the only car there, she breathed a sigh of relief. As long as Jilly was the next one to arrive, she was safe. Perhaps Jenny would decide to be fashionably late as a show of defiance. Perhaps she wouldn't show at all and only agreed to spite Grace since she still blamed her for 'influencing Bea against her.' She could only hope that wasn't the case.

As she sat there ruminating, Jilly pulled in and parked next to Grace. When she got out of her car, she rapped on Grace's window, startling her out of her reverie.

"You're early," Jilly said once Grace got out of her car.

They walked to the door together, Grace debating the best way to drop her little bomb.

"I need to talk to you about something," Grace said slowly. How did one announce they'd convinced someone's sworn enemy to help them?

Jilly unlocked the door, then turned to Grace, an expectant look on her face. "Yes?" she prompted. When Grace remained silent, Jilly gave her an exasperated sigh. "Come on, Grace, spit it out!"

The sound of a car door slamming nearby grabbed their attention, Jilly turning to see who was out and about so early in the morning. When Jenny appeared in the light from the streetlamp, she groaned.

"What is she doing here?" Jilly whispered to Grace.

Grace gulped. "That's what I was going to talk to you about," she admitted reluctantly. Why did she suddenly feel like she was in trouble? Asking Jenny to help out made so much sense yesterday. She truly was the only one in town with the experience to jump in without any training needed.

When Jenny reached them, she smiled smugly. "I knew it was only a matter of time before you failed," she gloated to Jilly. "If Bea had sold the business to me—like she should have—I would have everything under control."

"Is that so?" Jilly shot back. "So you're telling me you'd have no problem making HUNDREDS of cakes you've never made before with only a couple of DAYS' notice?" She folded her arms across her chest and stared back, her brow raised in challenge.

Jenny shifted uncomfortably but maintained eye contact. "What I'm saying is *I'd* never be desperate enough to beg *you* for help."

"Whoa, whoa," Grace said, holding out her hands between the women. "Ladies, we do not have time for this!" Grace reminded them. "We're on the same team, remember?" she said to Jenny specifically.

Jilly shook her head. "What are you two talking about?" she asked, her eyes narrowing in confusion. "When did I beg her for help, and why are you talking about us being a team?" she asked Grace.

"Why don't we go inside?" Grace asked, trying to buy some time. "It's freezing out here!"

"Finally, something we can all agree on," Jenny muttered.

Once they were inside, Jilly turned on the lights, set her purse and keys on the counter, then turned to Grace, an expectant look on her face.

Grace took a deep breath, then did her best to smile brightly. "I asked Jenny to help out, but only until the end of Mardi Gras," she explained. When Jilly's eyes widened, Grace held her hands out in a pleading motion. "I know you two don't get along, but she's the only one with the skills to fill in. I was desperate. I will help as much as I can, but once my guests arrive, I will be needed at the B&B and—"

"What's in it for you?" Jilly interrupted, turning her attention to Jenny. "Other than an opportunity to sabotage me, that is."

Jenny snorted. "You wish! I don't have to sabotage you; all I have to do is wait for the inevitable. Unlike you, I believe in earning my way to the top."

Jilly threw her hands up in frustration. "Ugh!!" she screamed. "Why do you insist on believing this narrative that I somehow screwed you out of a job? I barely even knew you when Bea agreed to sell me the bakery, and I would have gladly kept you on as my assistant!"

"**Assistant!**" Jenny screeched. "Why would *I* assist *you*? I'm the one who spent years working here! I know all the recipes, all the customers, the vendors, and everything in between. The only reason Bea gave you the bakery over me is because you have kids and she felt *sorry* for you!"

This did not seem like the time to tell Jenny that Bea never had any intention of selling the bakery to her. In fact, she had offered it to Tess before she settled on Jilly. Someday, she would have to convince Bea to have a heart-to-heart with Jenny and explain her reasoning. *If* Bea ever came back home.

Grace held out her hands as she, once again, stepped between them. "Look, we really do not have time for this. Today is the first full day of the carnival, and we only have a few hours until customers are going to be lined up outside the door. Can we please set aside our differences until AFTER we've survived the day?"

"Fine," Jilly shrugged. "I will if she will."

Jenny snatched an apron off a nearby hook and tied it around her waist. "I have no idea why I'm agreeing to this, but fine. What do you want me to do?"

"How about I keep working on the king cake recipes while you two get started on the donuts?" Grace suggested.

"I already have a king cake recipe," Jenny informed them. "I was planning to sell them on my social media page, but I've been busy and never got around to setting it up." She looked up to see them looking at her. "What? It's a lot of work. I have to figure out pricing, take pictures, make posts about it, yada yada yada."

All of that and more was part of running a business. Suddenly, Bea's decision not to sell to Jenny was starting to make sense. She was a great baker, but if she couldn't handle the most basic of business tasks, how would she handle running an entire bakery? Again, probably not the best time to point that out.

"Okay, then you work on the king cakes, and I'll make the donuts with Jilly," Grace offered. "If that's okay with you?" she asked Jilly.

Jilly nodded. "Works for me."

They got to work, each woman doing her best to ignore the others. This was not at all how Grace had hoped things would go, but she supposed it was better than what she'd feared.

***

Several hours passed, and by the time Grace checked her watch, it was almost eight.

"We're here!" Granny called out cheerfully as she, Gladys, Carl, and Katherine entered the kitchen.

Grace's head flew up at the sound of Granny's voice. "What are you doing here?" she asked, her mouth gaping in shock.

"We told you yesterday at the meeting we would help out," Granny reminded her.

"I mean, yeah, you did, but I didn't think you were serious," Grace replied. She didn't want to be rude, but working at the bakery was not for the faint of heart.

Gladys clucked her tongue. "Do not look at us like *that*, young lady. I'll have you know we've already served breakfast at the house *and* the hotel, *and* we've got plenty of energy left to serve that long line of customers waiting outside."

Grace slapped her forehead with the palm of her hand. "Oh my gosh, I forgot all about the hotel! Thank you for taking care of that." This was not good. She was already forgetting the most basic parts of her job, and her main guests hadn't even arrived yet. This was simply not acceptable.

"You're welcome," Granny said with a nod. "So do you want our help or not?"

Jilly gave them each a hug. "I would love your help," she replied. "But only if you're sure?" When they nodded, she continued, "If you can serve, we can keep baking back here. Let me show you how to work the register."

"No need," Gladys told her. "I've had plenty of practice over the years. You get back to work; we'll handle things up front."

Granny and Gladys made their way to the front of the store, leaving Carl and Katherine behind.

"What would you like us to do?" Carl asked.

Grace looked at the stack of king cakes Jenny spent the morning working on. "As our resident Mardi Gras experts, how about you be our official taste testers?"

"Hey, Grace?" Granny called out as she poked her head back in the kitchen. "Molly wanted me to remind you you're supposed to meet Stacey at the hotel this morning."

"Who's Stacey?" Grace asked, her brow furrowing. And why was she supposed to meet her at the hotel? Is this another guest Molly forgot to tell her about?

Granny shrugged. "I don't know, but you better get over there." She disappeared again, leaving Grace to figure it out on her own.

"Okay," Grace said, taking off her apron and hanging it on a nearby hook. "I guess I better go. Will you guys be okay without me?"

"Don't worry about us," Carl reassured her. "We'll stay here and do our best to help out. If we end up in the way, we'll go see what mischief we can get up to out there," he said, nodding toward the carnival.

Grace hated to leave them—but since she had no choice—she said goodbye and went outside, weaving through the throng of customers as she walked the hundred or so feet to the hotel, where the woman from yesterday was waiting outside. So that's Stacey. She supposed that should have been obvious, but she could have sworn the woman only planned to work while her kids were in school.

"It's nice to see you again," Grace said cheerfully as she held out her hand to the woman. She studied her more closely. She was about Grace's height, with long dark hair that was currently pulled back in a tidy braid, and expressive brown eyes framed by long, thick lashes. Had she seen her somewhere before? Grace couldn't recall. It was weird how you could live in such a small town and still run into people you've never met before. "I'll admit, I wasn't expecting you until Monday," Grace continued.

"My husband's with the kids," Stacey explained. "But if you'd prefer me to wait until Monday..."

"No, no, no," Grace interrupted. "I'm glad to have your help, really I am." She unlocked the door and motioned for Stacey to follow her inside. "Let me give you a quick tour before we get started on the cleaning."

By quick tour, she meant power walking through the lobby, dining room, and kitchen before grabbing the cleaning cart and heading toward the bathrooms. Luckily, Granny and Gladys had also cleaned up after breakfast in addition to serving it, so that was one less thing they had to worry about. She owed them, big time.

"Things sure are strange around here," Stacey commented as she looked around the women's bathroom.

Grace took in the retro-pink tiles and fixtures and grimaced. "We haven't gotten around to remodeling this part of the hotel," she explained.

Stacey gave her a quizzical look. "Oh, you thought I meant the décor," she said with a laugh. "While it is very pink, I wouldn't call it strange."

"Then what were you talking about?" Grace asked, genuinely curious. Winterwood was known to have her quirks, but no one had ever claimed it was strange before. At least, not to her knowledge.

"It's just..." Stacey hesitated a moment, as if unsure if she should continue. "On my way here, I walked through the carnival and saw a woman in a wedding dress—with a cast on her arm, as well as a man wearing a fancy Mardi Gras mask. I know it's Mardi Gras and all, but he was the only one, you know? And it just seemed...odd."

There was only one woman known to run around in wedding dresses: Shelley. Which meant she was surely up to something. All Grace could do now was hope she wasn't making a nuisance of herself with the carnival people—or doing something crazy that was bound to get herself, or someone else, hurt. Apparently, Grace's plan to convince

Shelley to take up acting had backfired. The man was a bit of a curveball, but maybe he really liked Mardi Gras. It wasn't a crime to wear a mask at a celebration, especially when there was a booth at said celebration selling those very masks. Maybe he was Lyda's first sale of the day.

"They sound like eccentric people," Grace finally replied. "That seems par for the course with events like this."

"Of course," Stacey said quickly. "I wasn't trying to offend. My family is new to the area, and we aren't used to this kind of thing."

That would explain why Grace had never seen her before. "Where are you from?" she asked as she finished wiping down the last mirror. It was now time for the toilets—or, as Grace liked to think of it, time to see what her new worker was made of. If she didn't take one look in the stalls and run screaming for the hills, she was a keeper for sure.

"A small town in Nebraska," Stacey said as she got to work in the first stall. "We've been looking for months for a place to move to that had a small-town feel, but actually had things to do, you know?"

No, she didn't know. Until recently, Winterwood had been as dull as the town Stacey had moved from. And honestly, Grace hadn't minded. Sure, she loved throwing these events, but she also loved the quiet times in between. Hopefully Stacey would feel the same way.

"It looks like we're done," Grace said as she stepped back and admired their work. "One down, one to go."

"Plus the rooms?"

Grace nodded. "Yes, but those should be quick. We just need to change the sheets today. We'll do a deeper clean on Monday, and then again on Friday after the guests check out."

"Sounds good to me," Stacey agreed. "Lead the way!"

Impressed by Stacey's enthusiasm, she led them to the first room. Things were looking up. She had the help she needed, Jilly had Jenny, and, well, as long as those two could get along for the next two weeks, everything would be okay. Right? Right!

-Nine-

G race served the last bowl of shrimp and grits and then took her seat between Granny and Cole. "So..." she asked the group, "What do you think?"

Carl took a bite, chewed thoughtfully for a moment, then grabbed a napkin and quickly raised it to his mouth. "It's good, but I think you forgot to remove the tails on the shrimp," he replied after a sip of water.

Katherine, Granny, Rebekah, and Cole put their spoons down and exchanged uncomfortable looks.

"You did de-vein the shrimp, right?" Rebekah asked, her face now sporting a tinge of green.

"Um," Grace said, pulling nervously at her shirt collar. "I don't remember that part in the instructions. Is that bad?"

Rebekah made a gagging noise before gulping down her glass of tea.

"I'll take that as a yes," Grace said dryly. "Looks like shrimp and grits is off the menu." She picked up as many bowls as she could carry and took them to the kitchen. Seconds later, she returned with a serving bowl of

Cajun corn and kale salad. "Try this," she instructed. "No shrimp, just vegetables and spices," she assured them.

When they didn't gag, she took that as a good sign and turned her attention to Granny. "I've been dying to know how it went at the bakery yesterday," she said. "Did Jenny and Jilly get along?"

Granny hesitated, then took a sip of tea before responding. "Let's just say the hatchet is far from buried."

"Unless you count Jenny burying it in Jilly's back," Katherine added.

Grace groaned. "Does that mean Jenny won't be helping out after all?" If that were the case, that meant she would be back on duty, and she simply did not have time for that.

"Last we heard, they'd called a temporary truce, but I wouldn't count on that lasting more than a few days tops," Granny replied.

"Great," Grace said, letting out a big sigh. "What do we do now?" She tried rearranging her schedule in her mind, but even with Stacey, that did not leave much time.

Carl cleared his throat. "Katherine and I have agreed to work the front of the bakery while Josie and Gladys help out in the kitchen. If anyone can keep Jilly and Jenny in line, it's those two."

This was just great. Carl and Katherine were supposed to be guests, not the hired help. Were they even getting paid for this? At the very least, she would have to refund their money for the Mardi Gras Experience, and even that might not be enough.

"The salad is a winner," Rebekah said, pushing back her bowl. "Not to change the subject, but we still need to decide if the ballroom at the hotel will work for the masquerade ball. Since you have a few minutes to spare today, I suggest we go over there and check it out."

"I can help clean up here and then meet you at home," Cole offered.

She hesitated. Today was supposed to be their official day off together, and here she was, about to work. If she made an exception this time, it would be that much easier to make them in the future, and they'd be right back to working seven days a week. But did she really have a choice?

"Okay, I'll be quick," Grace replied. She kissed his cheek, then followed Rebekah outside.

The drive to the hotel would have normally taken less than three minutes, but with the carnival in full swing, it took them ten to navigate the extra traffic. Grace briefly wondered how her neighbors felt about that but quickly dismissed that loaded question. Best not to borrow trouble.

They walked into the lobby, through the French doors to the dining room, then continued on through another set of French doors to the back of the hotel, where the ballroom was located. Once inside, Grace felt along the wall for the light switch, flipping it on once she found it. The bulbs flickered to life a few times, then went out, leaving them in darkness.

Grace sighed, walked over to the windows, and pulled back the curtains, the rod falling off the wall and bouncing on the floor, dust spewing up around her like a cloud. She did that a few more times—much more carefully, of course—until there was enough light for them to see gold-plated chandeliers with dangling crystals lining the middle of the room, dust-covered parquet wood floors, peeling damask wallpaper, and a stage at one end draped with moth-eaten heavy red curtains.

"I'm almost afraid to see what's behind those," Grace said, nodding toward the ruined fabric.

Rebekah raised a brow, then silently led the way, dragging Grace behind her.

When they reached the stage, they each grabbed a curtain and gingerly pulled it to the side, revealing more peeling wallpaper and dirty wood floors.

Grace took a step forward, her boot crashing through the wood. She flailed a moment before Rebekah reached out and grabbed her just in time to keep her from falling through the floor. "Thanks," Grace said, her voice shaky.

"I take it you didn't know about this?" Rebekah asked as she held Grace steady while she yanked her foot out of the hole she'd just created.

She shook her head. "Like I said the other day, we've only been in here once." She rubbed her leg, checking to make sure there were no cuts or splinters. "I probably should have at least cleaned in here once over the past year, but I never got around to it."

"Didn't the inspector catch it?"

That's right—they bought the hotel *before* Rebekah became a part of their lives, so she missed out on all the fun. "Grant and Molly passed on the inspection," Grace explained. When Rebekah made a face, Grace continued. "I felt the same way, but there were multiple offers on the place, and they thought it would make our offer more enticing if we gave up our right to an inspection."

"I guess they were right," Rebekah said dryly. "We better get someone out here to look at this, as well as the rest of the floor," she said, squinting at the wood through the dust and dirt. "It might be best to forget about this and use the community center like we'd originally planned."

"Are you sure?" Grace asked. "Shouldn't we wait to find out how bad things are before we make that decision?"

Rebekah gave her the side-eye. "Even if the rest of the floor is in perfect condition, this place is filthy, the wallpaper is peeling, and neither of us has time to fix that before the big event."

"We could always get a group of volunteers together to help us out..."

"While I typically appreciate your optimism, I think it's best we stop piling tasks on top of our already too-full plates. We don't need another Jilly and Jenny situation on our hands."

Grace winced. "I really messed up with that, didn't I?"

"I'm sure you had your reasons," Rebekah replied. "But the guests are scheduled to arrive tomorrow, so that needs to be our focus."

The urge to argue was strong, but Grace knew Rebekah was right. Unless... "I'll call Jim and ask him to come out tomorrow," Grace informed her. "Maybe I can time it so he'll get here before the guests arrive."

"I suppose that's fine, but only if you already plan to be here anyway," Rebekah replied.

They made their way back to the front of the hotel, pausing to take in the crowded carnival. A flash of white caught their eye, each of them turning just in time to see Shelley chasing a man in a mask through the maze of tents.

"Do I want to know what that's all about?" Grace asked.

"It's best if you don't."

***

Grace walked through the door of the farmhouse, then immediately bent down to give the dogs hugs and pets. When Max's big body accidentally knocked her over, she laughed as they began to lick her face.

Fweeeet

Ruby and Max jumped to attention at the sound of Cole's whistle.

"Bed!" he commanded as he bent down to help Grace up.

"My hero," Grace sang out as she batted her eyelashes at him. "What would I do without you?"

Cole grinned. "Probably become a chew toy!"

She rolled her eyes and playfully smacked him on the arm. "So what should we do today?" she asked as they walked hand in hand to the sofa and sat down.

Knock Knock

They exchanged surprised glances.

"Are you expecting someone?" Grace asked.

"No," he said with a shake of his head. "Are you?"

When she shook her head, he got back up and walked to the door.

Curious to see who it was, Grace leaned over so she could see around him, then immediately became anxious when she saw it was Riley. Was there a problem on the farm? Or was he here to tell them he's leaving? The thought of her worst fear coming true caused her heart rate to skyrocket, and she had to take several calming breaths to get it to slow back down. At some point, she really needed to figure out why she always jumped to the worst-case scenario and find a way to put a stop to it. This was no way to live.

"Hi, Riley," Grace called out. She gave a little wave, then motioned for him to come inside. "Can I get you something to drink?"

Riley shook his head, then took a seat in the chair opposite them. "I'm sorry to interrupt your day off," he told them. "But I need to talk to you, and I'm afraid it can't wait any longer."

This did not sound good. He really was going to quit, wasn't he?

Cole resumed his seat next to Grace and took her hand. "Is something wrong?" he asked Riley.

He cleared his throat a couple of times, then took his cowboy hat off and began to rotate the brim. "Katie's been accused of stealing money from the town," he said slowly. "She swears she didn't do it, that the real culprit has framed her, but so far they haven't been able to find any proof of that."

Grace took no pleasure in being right. "Who does she think is framing her?" There wasn't a single person she could think of who would do something like that, and other than Allen and Derek, who would even have the ability? Surely Katie didn't think one of them did it?

Riley lowered his gaze to the floor. "She accused Rebekah, and when she was informed Rebekah couldn't have done it, she accused you, Grace."

"Me?" Grace leaned forward, her hand pointing toward her chest. Had she heard him right? "But why?"

His lips moved, but no sound came out. Finally, he sighed and leaned back in the chair, his eyes raised to the ceiling. "She claims you did it to get rid of her so Rebekah could win me back."

"But that's ridiculous!" Grace practically shouted. "Rebekah is engaged to Thorne! And even if she wasn't, if she truly were looking for a way to win you back, I would never commit a crime to help her do that."

Cole wrapped his arm around her shoulders and pulled her close. "I highly doubt there's a single person who would believe you're capable of something like that," he said reassuringly.

She shook her head. Even if that were true, accusations like that had a way of following a person around.

"Emilio looked into it, but to my knowledge, he's cleared the entire town council at this point," Riley told her. "The only ones he hasn't been able to clear are Katie, and by extension me, though I am fully cooperating and hope to be cleared soon."

It took her a minute to process that. "Why is Emilio involved?"

Riley shrugged. "From what I gather, he has a background in forensic accounting."

That's why Molly and Grant knew what was going on. Things were starting to fall into place. "Wait, how did they clear us without asking us any questions?"

"You'll have to ask Emilio," Riley replied. "All I know is things are likely to get a lot worse before they get better, and I wanted you to hear it from me first."

Cole gave a polite nod. "I appreciate that. What can we do to help?"

Riley looked up, his eyes widening in surprise. "Um, nothing really. I was about to offer to quit, or at the least, take a leave of absence until this gets cleared up. I didn't want you to worry about whether or not you had a thief working for you."

Grace squeezed Cole's hand. She wanted to jump in and reassure the poor man but knew it was best to let Cole handle things.

"You and I have worked side by side every day for almost a year," Cole told him. "You were the best man at my wedding, the only man I trusted to run my farm while I was on my honeymoon, so I'd like to think I know a little something about trust, and as far as I'm concerned, you are as trustworthy as they come."

"In case that wasn't clear, we don't want you to leave," Grace interjected. She wiped the corner of her eye, moved by Cole's little speech. While it was true her motives for wanting Riley to stay were a tad on the selfish side, she wholeheartedly agreed with Cole; Riley was a good and honest man.

He gave them one of his lopsided smiles, clearly relieved they weren't kicking him to the curb. "Thanks, guys. I really appreciate your faith in me. But if you change your mind—"

"We won't," Grace hurried to assure him.

Riley laughed, then placed his hat back on his head and moved to the door, Grace and Cole following close behind.

"Where is Katie now?" Grace asked, curious as to just how serious things were.

"She's staying with her parents," he replied. "Right now she's only a person of interest, but she's been warned not to leave town until the investigation is complete."

That sounded very serious to Grace, but what did she know?

"I'll let y'all get back to your day off," Riley tipped his hat, then hopped into the farm cart and drove off toward the barn.

"What do you think of that?" Grace asked once they were seated again.

Cole studied her for a moment. "I think it's a sad situation all the way around," he said slowly. "If Katie's guilty, her life will change dramatically. If she's innocent, this experience is still likely to change her."

Grace nodded. "I think you're right. I don't wish ill on the woman, but her accusations are wild and not likely to win her many friends. Though I suppose she must have been pretty desperate when she made them."

"Let's just be thankful nothing came of them," he replied.

As far as that went, Grace was already a few steps ahead of him. She snuggled up against his chest, then surprised herself by yawning. "How about we take a quick nap and then spend the rest of the day eating pancakes and binge-watching our new show?"

"Sounds like a perfect way to spend our day!"

-Eight-

The big day was finally here: guest arrival day! She couldn't wait to meet her new guests and officially get the party started! But first, she needed to meet Jim at the hotel. And serve breakfast. And clean the rooms. And make sure drinks and snacks were ready and waiting when her guests began to arrive... Such was the life of a busy innkeeper!

Cole was in the kitchen making coffee when Grace joined him. "Good morning," she said, wrapping her arms around his waist as she kissed his cheek.

"Good morning," he said back. He studied her for a moment. "You seem, dare I say, less stressed than usual today."

Grace did a mental check, surprised to discover he was right—she did feel less stressed. Which was interesting, considering she was about to meet a handyman to discuss what could be major issues at the hotel. Maybe she was turning over a new leaf? "I guess I'm just excited," she said with a shrug. "Are you still planning to stay at Granny's with me tonight?"

"Of course," he replied. "Where you go, I go."

She smiled, then kissed his cheek again and let go. "I like the sound of that, Mr. Reed," she called over her shoulder. "I'll see you tonight!"

When she pulled into a parking spot in the back of the hotel, she glanced over to the bakery and saw the lights were on. Should she pop over and check on things? She checked her watch. Jim would be there any minute, so she would have to do it later. It's not like she would be able to help anyway.

Once inside, she rushed to the lobby and unlocked the door just in time to see Jim step out of his truck.

"Thanks for coming so early," she called out to him as she held open the door.

"Who needs sleep!" he quipped. When he saw the guilty look on her face, he smiled reassuringly. "I'm just teasing you. I'm usually up at this time getting the kiddo ready for school."

Grace led him to the ballroom, pausing to turn on the lights before remembering they didn't work. "We'll have to use the flashlights on our phones," she said apologetically.

They turned them on, then slowly made their way to the stage, Grace shining her light on the spot where her foot went through the floor.

Jim bent down to examine the wood, brushing away some of the dust to see better. "It would be helpful if we could get this cleaned up," he told her. "From what I can tell so far, the damage looks like it was caused by termites, but I'll need to do a much closer inspection to tell for sure."

She didn't know what termites were, but they didn't sound good. "What else could it be?" she asked, hopeful there was a better alternative.

"Water damage," he replied, his focus on the spot where he shined his phone's flashlight. He looked up at the ceiling, then shook his head. "But I don't see any obvious signs of that. However, in order for the termites to survive, there has to be a water source close by."

"Are you saying the damage is new?" she asked in surprise. She had just assumed by how brittle the wood had been that the damage was old. Like, decades old.

He shrugged. "No way to know until I can get in there. I know this is a big ask, but if you can get this place cleaned up by this afternoon, I can come back and do a proper inspection."

That was a big ask, but not impossible. If Stacey was willing to help, they could probably get it done between breakfast and check-in. Which brought to mind another question—was it safe? The last thing she needed was for one of them to fall through the floor and get hurt.

"Um, what about that?" Grace asked, pointing to the hole.

Jim looked at the hole again, then up at her. "Stick to the outer perimeter and you should be fine. But if the floor starts to feel soft, give it a wide berth, okay?"

They walked back to the lobby, Grace pausing at the door. "Worst-case scenario, how long do you think it would take to make the needed repairs?"

His lips pursed as he considered her question. "Absolute worst case? At least a month, maybe two."

Grace wrinkled her nose. "Best case?"

"A week, but I wouldn't count on that," he cautioned.

"But there's hope?" Grace pressed, unwilling to give up just yet.

He smiled at her, then opened the door. "I'll see you this afternoon," he called over his shoulder, refusing to answer her question.

She watched him leave, then hurried to the kitchen to start breakfast for the carnival crew. Her to-do list had just grown significantly, but her excitement was holding strong. To her, that alone was a win!

***

Grace made it back to the B&B with just enough time to arrange the fruit and veggie platters before her first guests arrived. Cleaning the ballroom hadn't been as bad as she'd expected. It had taken a while to find a ladder tall enough to reach the chandeliers, but once she'd managed that, changing the lightbulbs had been pretty straightforward. The added light made a HUGE difference, instantly transforming the room from drab to—well, not exactly fab. It was still dirty, and the wallpaper was still peeling, but the potential was there.

Thanks to Stacey's brilliant idea to use the hose attachments on the vacuums, they'd managed to clean the floors in no time. Well, they were clean enough anyway.

She wouldn't eat off them, but Jim would at least be able to see what he was dealing with now.

To her surprise, the floors looked to be in great shape. There were no obvious signs of damage—at least to her untrained eye—and as far as she was concerned, all they needed was a good polishing and waxing, and they'd be good as new! The stage had been another matter entirely, and she could feel her anxiety start to creep in whenever she thought about it. However, she was doing her best to keep it at bay.

Ding Dong

She looked up from the king cake she was slicing—a delicious strawberry and cream cheese confection she'd made herself—and hurried over to the door.

"Welcome to the Enchanted Holiday Hideaway!" Grace exclaimed as she threw open the door.

The words were a bit of a mouthful, but she still loved saying them.

The couple on the porch smiled, the man extending his hand. "You must be Grace," he said, pumping her hand enthusiastically. "I'm Phillip, and this is my wife Eva." He gestured toward the woman next to him, who looked up from her phone long enough to give a small wave, then turned her attention back to the screen.

It was clear from his strained expression Phillip was not happy, but Grace did her best to ignore the awkwardness. "Follow me and I'll show you to your room," she told them.

As they walked through the foyer and up the stairs, Grace gave her usual spiel about the history of the house, pointing out all the woodwork and fancy moldings. When they reached the hallway, she showed them the bathroom, then led them to their room. Since it was winter, and more than a little chilly out, she'd started a low fire in the fireplace, the flames providing heat that was both cozy and inviting. On the table between the two chairs in front of it sat their welcome gift of a king cake, a bottle of chilled sparkling cider, plus two champagne flutes.

Eva put her phone down on the table and took it all in, walking around the room as she ran a finger over all the surfaces. "It matches the pictures," she said. She walked over to the fireplace and took a seat in one of the chairs. "What's this?" she asked, pointing to the cake.

"It's a king cake," Grace replied, somewhat taken aback by the less-than-enthusiastic look on the woman's face. "It's a Mardi Gras tradition."

"I don't eat sugar," she said, pushing the cake toward the other side of the small table.

The sound of footsteps thundering up the stairs caught Grace's attention, and she excused herself, grateful for the chance to leave. Once she was back out in the hallway, she caught Shelley making a beeline for her room.

"What on earth is going on?" Grace whispered.

"Tell him I'm not home," Shelley replied, her breath coming in short gasps.

"Tell who?" Grace asked. She looked over her shoulder, but there was no one there.

Ding Dong

"Him," Shelley said as she dove into her room and slammed the door.

This day was getting weirder by the minute.

Grace raised her hand to knock on Phillip and Eva's door, intent on telling them about the fruit and veggie platters before she went back downstairs, but stopped when she heard their raised voices.

"We promised we would unplug, remember?" Phillip said to Eva. *"But you've been on your phone since we left the house!"*

Eva let out an exasperated sigh. *"Would you give it a rest already? We just got here. Everyone knows travel days don't count toward the vacation."*

Ding Dong Ding Dong

Afraid she'd get caught eavesdropping, Grace hurried downstairs. It looked like her first guests could use some of the enchanted part of their holiday hideaway. She'd just have to figure out how to make that happen.

"Welcome to the Enchanted Holiday Hideaway!" Grace said enthusiastically as she threw open the door once more.

A man in a Mardi Gras mask stood on the porch, a suitcase on either side of him.

Was this the man Shelley was running from? Hadn't she seen Shelley chasing a man similar to this just yesterday? What was going on?

"I'm Jack," he said, holding out his hand.

Remembering her manners, Grace shook his hand, then stepped back to allow him entry. So the mystery man was also one of her guests, it would seem. It would also seem that Shelley was unaware of that particular fact. Things were about to get interesting—that much was for sure.

"Allow me to show you to your room," Grace offered, unsure of what else to do.

They went upstairs, Jack quizzing her the whole way.

"How many people live here?" he asked.

"There will be eleven in total once all the guests have arrived," Grace replied.

"How many of the eleven are guests?"

No one had ever asked that before, though she supposed that was a valid question. "Eight," Grace told him, stopping just outside his door. She turned the knob, then motioned him inside. This was one of the smaller rooms, but it was still decorated nicely, and while it didn't have a fireplace, she had still provided a king cake and sparkling cider.

"So that means there are three people who live here full-time?"

These questions were starting to make her uncomfortable. "Yes, my grandmother, myself, and my husband." She put extra emphasis on the word 'husband,' just in case.

It was hard to tell through the mask, but he seemed disappointed by her response. It was also awkward that he hadn't taken it off. She could understand him wearing it as a sign of his enthusiasm, but did he plan to wear it the whole time?

Ding Dong

"That should be the remaining guests," Grace told him. "Dinner will be served at six in the dining room downstairs. There are snacks and drinks on the breakfast bar, and if you need anything else, I'll be around all day."

Jack nodded, then shut the door with a soft click.

Grace was just about to head back downstairs when Shelley popped her head outside her door.

"What are you doing?" she asked in a loud whisper. "I told you to tell him I'm not here, not show him to a room!"

"He's a paying guest," Grace whispered back. "I couldn't very well turn him away. Besides that, why are you even running from him in the first place?"

Shelley rolled her eyes. "Duh, he's an obsessed fan. I prefer my fans to stay on the other side of the screen, thank you very much."

Ding Dong

"I need to get that," Grace told her. "Stay in your room for now, and when I get back, we'll come up with a plan, okay?"

She shook her head and bolted from the room. "No way am I staying up here alone—I've seen the movies. I'm going back to campaigning. *You* can figure out how to keep *me* safe while I'm gone and let me know when I get back."

Once they reached the front door, Shelley shook her finger at Grace. "You better not cheap out on the solution either. At the very least, there better be armed guards outside my door."

Shelley flung open the door and sashayed past the couple waiting there.

"Is she wearing a wedding dress?" the woman asked.

Grace inwardly groaned. She'd become so accustomed to Shelley and her white dresses they no longer registered. "She's..." how do you explain someone like Shelley to the non-initiated? "eccentric," Grace finally said. "Welcome to the Enchanted Holiday Hideaway!" she added quickly, hoping to distract them.

Buzz Buzz

As she led them inside, she pulled her phone out of her back pocket and checked her messages, the one from Jim lighting up her screen.

Hey Grace, can we postpone the inspection till tomorrow morning, same time?

Sure, that works better for me anyway.

She put her phone back in her pocket and led them upstairs, wondering all the way if they would be unimpressed like Eva had been. When they reached their room, she showed them inside, then held her breath as she waited for their reaction.

"It's beautiful!" the woman gushed as she took it all in. "I just love the canopy bed, and this fire is divine!" She plopped down in a chair in front of the fireplace, then noticed the cake and cider. "Is this for us?"

Grace smiled and nodded, thankful at least someone appreciated her efforts. "I'm Grace, by the way," she said, just now remembering she'd been so distracted by Shelley she'd failed to introduce herself. "And you must be Dwayne and Jasmine!"

"Guilty as charged!" Jasmine joked.

Dwayne groaned but smiled lovingly at his wife. "Forgive my wife, she's corny, but I love her anyway!"

When Grace gave them a curious look, Dwayne explained, "Jasmine works for the police department and loves to make police-themed jokes."

That was comforting. If Jack really was a stalker—or worse—they had help right here in the house. But she hoped it would never come to that. Knowing Shelley, it was all some weird misunderstanding anyway, though that did not explain the questions he asked earlier. However, it was entirely possible those questions were innocent and Grace simply took them the wrong way due to Shelley's drama.

She repeated her earlier spiel about snacks and dinner, then left them to unpack. This new group was certainly different from any other group she'd hosted. It would be interesting to see how things went the next day when their vacation 'officially' started.

-Seven-

G race had just finished setting up the breakfast buffet at the hotel when Jim walked in.

"Good morning," she called out. "Help yourself to a plate if you're hungry. There's plenty for everyone." She meant it, too. She'd somehow managed to make double what she was used to, but that just meant she'd have plenty to take back to the B&B.

"I'm good, but thanks," Jim replied. "Did you get those floors cleaned up?"

She nodded, then followed him back to the ballroom. "As you can see, the main floor looks pretty good," she said, waving her hands like Vanna White to showcase the floor. "The stage, on the other hand, is another story entirely."

Jim whistled when he saw the damage. "Definitely termites. From the look of things, they've been busy for a long time."

"So you think they're still active?" She'd spent part of last night researching the critters, and while she wouldn't consider herself an expert, she knew a lot more than she had the day before.

"It's definitely possible," he replied. "I'll know for sure once I start tearing out boards." He looked up at her. "If you decide to move forward with the repairs."

Grace couldn't think of a single reason why she wouldn't. If the infestation was active, they needed to stop it before it spread to other parts of the hotel. If it wasn't, she still wanted to be able to use the ballroom—not to mention the liability factor, since a guest could wander in here at any time and get hurt.

"Where are we at on the 'worst case versus best case' scenario?" she asked instead.

"That depends on whether the termites are active and how close you want to come to matching the original floor."

If it were up to her, she wouldn't bother with that. Yes, she preferred restoration to remodeling, but this was just a stage in a room rarely used. She'd rather save those efforts for something that mattered. Unfortunately, it wasn't up to her, at least not only her. She would have to talk to Molly and Grant and allow them to weigh in on the decision. And Cole. She should probably include him in this too, now that they were married.

"How about I go talk to my partners while you work up an estimate," she proposed. "I know they're going to want to know numbers and time frames, so how soon do you think you can get that over to me?"

Jim checked his watch. "Give me a couple of hours and I'll send them over."

"Perfect, that should give me enough time to finish my to-do list."

She walked him to the lobby and was about to go back to the dining room when she saw Jilly come flying out of the bakery and over to Jim, a frantic look on her face. Grace watched them talk, curious as to what was going on. She couldn't hear what they were saying, but could tell by Jilly's expression that whatever it was, it wasn't good.

While she debated going out to offer assistance, the two of them went their separate ways—Jilly back to the bakery while Jim roared off in the opposite direction. Movement caught her eye, and when she turned to see what it was, she saw Jack watching from the opposite corner, his mask in place. Or was it Jack? She really had no way of knowing for sure. All she knew was that something strange was going on, and she needed to get to the bottom of it as soon as possible.

***

Back at the B&B, Grace rushed to get breakfast laid out before her guests came down. There was a little of everything, so even the pickiest of eaters should be able to find something they liked—including Miss I-don't-eat-sugar, who she just knew was going to have a problem with something if last night's dinner had been any indication.

Eva had spent at least fifteen minutes grilling Grace on the meal she prepared. Were the ingredients fresh? Were they organic? Which country were they from? Like, it's winter in the middle of the rural Midwest—what did she expect? But hey, today is her official first day of vacation, so maybe things will be different? One can only hope.

To her surprise, Jack was one of the first ones down, his mask still in place. He really was going to wear that thing non-stop, wasn't he? She studied the mask, searching for clues it was the same one she saw the man on the corner wearing, but quickly realized she had no idea what she was looking for. She would have to come up with an excuse to take a picture so she'd have something more concrete to go off next time. Assuming there was a next time.

Phillip and Eva came down next. She took one look at the buffet and turned her nose up. "I'll take oatmeal with blueberries, one piece of toast, lightly buttered—make sure it's sourdough, real sourdough, none of that imitation junk—and coffee, black."

Grace was not a short-order cook, but she had no desire to start the day off with a fight, so she did as requested. Luckily, she'd bought a loaf of 'real' sourdough bread from the bakery the other day. She would have to remember to ask Jilly for another loaf since she had no doubt this would become a recurring incident.

As Grace was finishing up Eva's breakfast, Dwayne and Jasmine came down, which left Shelley—but she was so unpredictable, it was impossible to guess when she would show up.

"Where are the others?" Jack asked once everyone was seated.

"Down at the local bakery," Grace explained, assuming he was referring to Granny, Gladys, Carl, and Katherine.

Jack looked at her, but it was impossible to tell what he was thinking since she couldn't see his face.

"Are we required to work while we're here?" he asked, his tone laced with disapproval.

It had never once crossed her mind someone would think that, but now that they had, she could see why. "Of course not," she hurried to assure him. "They simply volunteered to help out a friend, that's all."

"I guess that makes sense," he said reluctantly. "That explains where they are. Where are the others?"

Grace really did not appreciate him giving her the third degree. What business was it of his where everyone was? It was her B&B, not his. At no point did he need to know the location of anyone other than her, and even then, that was only so she could provide the services they'd paid for. Then it hit her—he was likely referring to Shelley, since, other than Cole, she was the only one missing. Maybe he really was an obsessed fan.

"I'm not sure," Grace hedged, unwilling to give up Shelley's whereabouts just in case this guy really was bad news. "I'm sure they'll be around later."

"These pancakes are the best I've ever had," Jasmine moaned. "The only thing better would have been donuts!"

Dwayne covered his face with his hands and groaned. "Surely you can do better than that tired joke," he teased.

Jasmine considered that. "Are you telling me not to quit my day job?" She tried to keep a straight face, but failed, her smile too big to be contained.

Eva looked at them and rolled her eyes. "I don't get it."

"How about we discuss the events of the day?" Grace said, changing the subject to one that was more positive. She left the table to grab their wristbands, handing one to each of them when she returned. "These are good for the entire day," she explained. "You can use them to go on the rides as many times as you want, to get into the shows, and for one free donut at the bakery. I will have a new one for you tomorrow, so don't worry about saving them once you're done for the day."

"What if we don't want to go to the carnival?" Jack asked as he turned his wristband over and over in his hands.

Grace eyed him a moment, to no avail. She simply could not get a read on the guy. "You are welcome to stay here and hang out. We have board games in the cabinet in the living room, as well as streaming services on all the televisions. There's a library down the street, a boutique on Main Street, as well as a coffee shop, a flower shop, and a general store if you want to do some shopping. If none of that interests you, the closest major city is about an hour away."

Jack grunted. "I have no desire to spend my day driving. Carnival it is," he said with a sigh.

Had Molly actually vetted this guy? Or did she drop the ball again? Why was he even here if he wasn't interested in any of the activities she'd planned? It's not like they were a secret.

"Well, I, for one am looking forward to it!" Jasmine exclaimed. "I can't remember the last time I went to a carnival. Why, I must have been a little girl!" Her face momentarily fell. "There won't be clowns, will there?"

"No clowns," Grace assured her. She clapped her hands together in an effort to stir up some excitement. "Alright, everyone, if you're ready to go, I'll walk you down there."

"In the cold?" Eva asked, her face scrunched in distaste.

Maybe she should have brought one of Cole's farm vehicles over; then she could have ferried them down there. Oh well, she would talk to him about that later.

"Some of the tents are heated, so if you get cold, you can always step inside one of those," Grace informed them. "And don't forget about the coffee shop and other businesses. They would be happy to have you if you need a place to warm up for a while."

"You mean they would be happy to have our money," Jack sneered.

What was this guy's problem? At this point, she was willing to give him a refund and send him on his way. Even Eva and her demands were better than him. But she wasn't about to tell him that here. No, she would let Cole deal with him later—or perhaps Grant and Molly.

"I'll meet you all in the foyer in fifteen minutes," Grace told them. While they got ready, she cleared the table, then sent Cole a quick text.

'Can you meet me at Molly's office in thirty minutes?'

She watched the screen as three little dots appeared.

'Only if you really need me to. I'm in the middle of a situation.'

Of course he was.

'Never mind, we can talk tonight.'

Can't say she didn't try, right?

After she dropped the group off at the fortune teller's booth, she backtracked to Molly's office, waving to Tess on her way to see Molly.

"What's up?" Molly asked as Grace dropped into a chair.

"I need to talk to you and Grant," Grace replied.

Molly shifted uncomfortably. "He's not available right now. What do you need?"

Grace shook her head. "I know about Katie, okay? So we can stop all this secret, clandestine stuff."

"Who told you?" Molly asked, her eyes narrowed. "Because if it was Gladys, she and I are going to have a long talk tonight..."

"It was Riley," Grace admitted. "I'm pretty sure Cole and I are the only ones he's told, so don't worry about the news spreading around town."

She was silent for a moment, as if assessing whether Grace was telling the truth or lying to protect Gladys. "Is that why you're here? To discuss Katie?" she finally asked.

"Actually, no. I'm here to discuss the hotel. We found termite damage in the ballroom, and I need your approval to get it repaired."

"Who's we?" Molly asked. "And why is this the first time I'm hearing about this?"

Sometimes having partners really sucked. Like now, when she was forced to defend herself like she was a naughty child who got caught with her hand in the cookie jar. "'We' as in me and Rebekah, although Jim made the official diagnosis. And you're just now hearing about it because *I* just found out about it. Now can we get it fixed or not?" she snapped.

Molly's eyes widened at Grace's tone. "Wow, someone's in a mood. I need numbers and an estimate of how long it will take before I can make that decision."

"I'm two steps ahead of you," Grace said as she forwarded Molly the estimate from Jim. She played on her phone while she waited for Molly to look over the information. She supposed she probably should have looked, too, but was more interested in beating that day's Wordle puzzle than how much this latest fiasco would set them back financially.

When fifteen minutes had passed and Molly still hadn't made a decision, Grace began to get antsy. She still had the hotel to clean—not to mention the dishes from breakfast at the B&B, as well as lunch to cook and dinner to prepare. Plus, she needed to find Rebekah and arrange to get a booth set up so the town could vote for the Mardi Gras Queen and King.

"I'm willing to agree to the cheapest option," Molly finally announced. "I don't like the fact he can't make any guarantees at this time, so I would like you to have him call me with updates so I can monitor the project."

Grace wanted to protest—she was more than capable of doing that herself—but decided not to. She had enough to do. If Molly wanted to be the boss, so be it. "Sounds good," Grace said as she stood and prepared to leave. She had one foot out the door when she turned back one last time. "I plan to ask Jack to leave tonight. He's not a good fit for the group, and quite frankly, he's creeping me out."

"You can't!" Molly practically shouted. She took a breath, then tried again. "I'm sorry, I shouldn't have yelled. But my first response stands—you can't do that."

"Why not?"

"Because..." She looked up at the ceiling as if searching for divine inspiration. "Because you just can't."

This made no sense. While Molly was a business partner, this was still Grace's home, and if she wanted someone to leave, she had every right to ask them to. More importantly, why was Molly siding with some strange man instead of her friend?

"Look, Grace, I know I haven't been very forthcoming as of late, and I'm sorry for that. But please understand there are things going on you aren't aware of."

"And whose fault is that?" Grace shot back.

"I deserved that," Molly said as she winced. "But I promise you Jack is not a danger to you, okay? In time, everything will make sense."

Grace wasn't sure she believed her, but at least she would get her ballroom in time for the Masquerade Ball, barring any more unforeseen circumstances. She would just have to take the wins where she could, make lemonade out of lemons, yada yada yada.

"Fine, I'll see you at dinner tonight," Grace said, her tone brokering no argument—which was something she'd ironically learned from Molly. The student had finally become the master, as they say.

"See you tonight," Molly said, her voice fading as Grace walked away.

Yep, this was turning out to be one interesting event. And honestly, she was curious to see what happened next.

-Six-

Breakfast was just about ready when Rebekah walked through the door, a clipboard piled high with paper in her hands.

"To what do I owe the pleasure of your company?" Grace asked, her eyes twinkling with mischief as a smile tugged at her lips.

"Is that your way of saying you've missed me?" Rebekah asked dryly. "Because I'm pretty sure we've seen each other every day this week."

"Yes, but only for a few minutes," Grace replied, her smile replaced with a pout. "We haven't hung out since before my wedding, and well, I miss my friend."

Rebekah threw her arm around Grace's shoulders. "I miss you, too, but we'll have plenty of time to hang out once this event is over. In fact, we should plan a girls' day out. After all this work, we deserve a day of pampering!"

Speaking of work... "There's a chance the ballroom will be ready in time for the ball!" Grace exclaimed. "Only the stage needs to be repaired, and Jim is supposed to start work on it today."

Rebekah's eyes turned heavenward. "I should have known you would go forward with that even though we agreed there wasn't time."

"But—"

She held up her hand to silence her. "No buts," Rebekah said firmly. "I love how ambitious you are, but Grace, we have exactly one week until the ball. The volunteers have already begun decorating the community center, tickets are being sold as we speak with the community center as the location, and I simply cannot change all of that at the last minute! Not for a definite, but especially not for a 'chance' the ballroom will be ready."

"It's only two blocks down the street from the community center," Grace protested. "We could easily put signs directing people to the new location."

"Even if that is true, there's still the issue of parking we never solved, not to mention the number of people who will be confused and upset by this. Besides that, what are we supposed to do about decorating? We can't magically move the decorations from one building to the next in the blink of an eye, you know. Nor can the band move all their equipment, the catering—"

"Okay, fine, I get it," Grace interrupted. "You and your logic," she muttered.

Rebekah laughed, then reached over the counter and patted Grace's hand. "How about this—since it means so much to you—we'll come up with a reason to use the ballroom at a later time. Maybe we can offer to host the high school prom this year, or hold another murder mystery dinner, but this time, it will be contained to the hotel. Sort of like—what do you call them—a locked room mystery..." She waved her hand dismissively. "We'll come up with something."

Grace didn't hate the idea. The murder mystery she'd hosted last Valentine's Day had been fun, if not a little chaotic. She could definitely see the potential of hosting one in the hotel. Maybe it could be a weekend thing, a live-action game of Clue!

"Earth to Grace," Rebekah called out, waving her hand in front of Grace's face.

"Sorry," Grace said, blinking a few times as her mind drifted back to the present. "I was just imagining myself as Ms. Scarlet."

"As in, O'Hara?" Rebekah's brow furrowed. "How on earth ... never mind, we need to get back to the reason I'm here."

Jack walked in, followed by Eva, Phillip, Jasmine, and Dwayne.

"Who do we have here?" Jack asked, it clear even through his mask he was giving Rebekah an appraising look.

To her credit, Rebekah barely glanced in his direction. Instead, she stepped to the side to give them space to grab their breakfast, waiting patiently for everyone to finish and move to the dining table—which everyone did, except for Jack.

"Is there something I can help you with?" Grace asked him, her normally friendly tone now tinged with ice.

Jack cocked his head to the side. "Don't you think it's rude not to introduce me to your friend?"

"No," Grace replied. "I think it's rude to insist on an introduction when none has been freely offered."

He surprised her by laughing, the sound deep and rich. "Touché!" He grabbed his plate, then gave them a formal bow. "Ladies," he said, before taking his seat at the table.

"What was that about?" Rebekah whispered.

"Honestly, I have no idea," Grace whispered back. She studied the man for a moment, but no revelations came. When she looked back at Rebekah, she too was watching him, a curious expression on her face. "What is it?"

Rebekah continued to stare. "He seems familiar, but I can't for the life of me see why. Does he ever take off that mask? I would love to get a look at his face."

Grace shook her head. "At this point I think he sleeps in it," she joked. "Which is kind of weird, don't you think? Not that he sleeps in it—I mean that he's always wearing it. What is he hiding? Though sleeping in it is also weird. If he actually does. Which I obviously don't know. I don't spy on guests while they're sleeping. I—"

"Grace!" Rebekah squeezed her hand as she tried to get her attention. "What has gotten into you this morning?" she asked with a laugh.

"What?" she asked, genuinely confused.

"Never mind, we need to talk about this king and queen business, and I only have a few minutes before I need to be downtown," Rebekah told her. "We need to announce the winner before the parade on Saturday, so I think we should do that at the concert tomorrow night. Are you good with that?"

That would only give the winners a day and a half to find outfits for the parade, but Grace supposed that was better than nothing. She would have to remember to talk to Chrissy and Lyda and see if they could help come up with something so this wouldn't become a burden on the two lucky people. Thankfully, Lyda would be here in about twenty minutes, which solved half her problem.

"I think that works," Grace replied, still working out the logistics in her mind. "Any idea if Shelley's campaign efforts are proving fruitful...?"

Rebekah snorted. "Not a chance. The candidates are nomination-only, and poor Shelley hasn't even made the ballot yet, but that will likely change when she realizes she can nominate herself." She checked her watch. "I need to get going. Do you need anything from me before I go?"

"A hug," Grace replied. The words had flown out of her mouth instinctively, surprising even her.

"Aww." She set her clipboard down on the counter and wrapped her arms around Grace's neck. "It's going to be okay," she whispered. "And if you want to spy on mask guy while he's sleeping, let me know. I'm always up for a clandestine operation!"

Grace chuckled, then let go and wiped her eyes. "I just might take you up on that!"

Once Rebekah left, Grace wandered over to the table to check on her guests, relieved to see they were almost done with their breakfast.

"So what's on the agenda for today?" Jasmine asked. She licked the syrup off her fork, then stabbed a strawberry, rolling her eyes when Eva made a face at her. "I'm on vacation," she told her. "Vacation calories don't count. And even if they do, I don't care. I work too hard not to enjoy the rare time off I get."

Eva held up her hands. "Far be it from me to judge you," she snarked. "Wouldn't want to get a ticket for interfering in an active eating investigation."

Jasmine burst into laughter, then laughed even harder when Eva joined in. By the time they'd composed themselves, there were tears in their eyes.

For their part, the men were equal parts amused, bewildered, and annoyed.

Ding Dong

Drat, that could only be Lyda, and Grace hadn't cleaned up from breakfast yet. She went to answer the door, jumping into action when she saw the boxes Lyda was juggling begin to fall.

"You could have asked me to come outside and help," Grace told Lyda.

Lyda shrugged, the movement jostling the remaining boxes. "I thought I had it." She followed Grace inside, then plopped her stuff down on the end of the table opposite the diners. "Good morning, everyone! Are you ready to make a Mardi Gras mask? Or, as the French like to say, 'faire un masque de Mardi Gras?'" She eyed Jack. "Looks like one of you brought his own."

"Oh, I assumed he'd already visited your booth," Grace replied. That meant Jack had always planned to hide behind a mask while he was here. Things were getting stranger by the minute.

"I'm a 'go big or go home' kind of guy," Jack quipped. "If I'm going to celebrate, I'm going all the way."

"I bet you're popular at Christmas," Eva drawled.

"And Valentine's Day," Jack quipped.

Grace chose to ignore that and began clearing the dishes. For once, she planned to join her guests in their planned activity and was excited to get started. She just wished Cole could be here too. Maybe Lyda would be willing to make one for him if she wasn't too busy helping the others.

"I'm already a step ahead of you," Lyda replied when Grace asked. She pulled an exquisite mask out of one of the boxes and handed it to her to inspect.

"This is amazing!" Grace gushed. "Now I'm jealous. There's no way I can make something anywhere close to this nice."

"Why don't you try, and we'll see what you come up with?" Lyda encouraged. "If you truly aren't happy when you're done, I have a box full of masks you can choose from." She accepted Cole's mask from Grace and put it back in the box.

Lyda made short work of handing out the supplies, and before too long, the table was laden with an assortment of brightly colored feathers, gems, glitter, paint, and sequins, plus all the tools one could ever need to apply them. As far as arts and crafts went, this was on a whole other level.

Jack pushed his chair back and stood. "Since I don't need one of these, I think I'll head back down to the carnival. So, if you'll excuse me..." When no one protested, he took his leave, the front door slamming shut behind him.

"What is with that guy?" Jasmine asked once he was gone. "It seems awfully suspicious he refuses to take off that mask."

"I agree," Phillip said, his eyes on the paint as he chose a color. "I've even seen him wearing it to and from the bathroom. Like, who does that?"

Eva wrinkled her nose. "He's probably just doing it for the attention. He's the only one here without a partner—maybe he thinks the mask will help him with the ladies."

"Ohh, I see," Jasmine replied. "Like it makes him all tall, dark, and mysterious."

"Exactly!"

Given the interest Jack had shown first in Shelley, then in Rebekah, Grace thought they might be onto something with their theory. That did not explain Molly's insistence the man had to stay, but maybe the two were unrelated.

The banter continued as everyone focused on the task at hand, occasionally pausing to ooh and aah over each other's masks, every once in a while Lyda answering questions or doling out advice. When Grace had finished her mask, she had to admit it wasn't half bad—which also meant it wasn't half good either—but she wouldn't be embarrassed to wear it around town. As long as she wasn't standing next to Cole. She still had every intention of taking Lyda up on her offer for Grace to choose one of the pre-made masks to wear to the ball.

BAM!

Grace jumped at the sound, but before she could get up to see what had caused it, Shelley came storming into the room.

"YOU!" she shouted, pointing at Grace. "I warned you not to run against me, but you just couldn't help yourself, could you?"

"I have no idea what you're talking about," Grace told her, "but there better not be a hole in my wall from you slamming the door open."

Shelley glared at Grace, her nostrils flaring. "This. Means. WAR!" She took off one of her white gloves and threw it down on the table. "I am officially throwing down the jauntlet!"

"I think you mean gauntlet," Jasmine corrected.

She rolled her eyes. "Whatever, you know what I mean."

"Actually, I have no idea what you mean," Grace told her. "Are we supposed to arm wrestle? Play tug-of-war? Duel at dawn? And again, why are we fighting?"

"I'm talking about the Mardi Gras Queen!" Shelley said through gritted teeth. "As I'm sure you already know, you are beating me by a country mile, but that is about to change! It's time to bring in the big guns, and they are blazing!"

Shelley stomped out of the room, but was back seconds later. "I need that," she said, grabbing her glove from the middle of the table. "It's cold out there." She sneered at Grace, then left again, this time the door slamming behind her.

Why had Grace ever agreed to let that woman stay here?

"I wonder what she meant by 'big guns'?" Jasmine asked. "She didn't mean real guns, did she?"

Grace shook her head. "Shelley is dramatic, but harmless. She was probably referring to her parents."

"You seem to have missed the part where she said you're beating her for the title of Mardi Gras Queen," Lyda pointed out. "Aren't you the least bit excited about that?"

How had she missed that? And who nominated her? She certainly didn't nominate herself. "I can't be the queen," she protested. "I'm the one hosting the event."

"People might think you rigged the election," Jasmine agreed.

Eva looked down her nose at Grace. "Did you rig it?"

"Of course not!" Grace exclaimed. "I didn't even know there was such a thing as a Mardi Gras queen until just a few days ago." She put her face down on the table and groaned. "This is just great. Now everyone is going to think I'm a cheater."

"Or, since the townspeople are the ones voting, perhaps they just really want to see you as their queen," Lyda pointed out. "You are the town sweetheart, after all."

Grace's head shot up. "That's a brilliant idea! All I have to do is go to the voting booth and nominate someone else—someone everyone loves and respects. Then all my problems will be solved!" She jumped out of her chair and rushed toward the door. "Thanks, Lyda! You're a lifesaver!"

"Wait! That's not what I meant!" Lyda called after her. But it was no use—Grace was already gone.

Days till Mardi Gras

-Five-

G race was finishing up the last of the breakfast dishes when Jack appeared behind her, blocking her path. Startled, she jumped back against the sink, bumping her hip against the dishwasher door.

"Sorry," he said as he reached out a hand to steady her.

She waved him off, suddenly aware that they were the only two people in the house, the rest of the guests having already left for the day. "Did you need something?" she asked curtly.

Jack cocked his head to the side, then leaned nonchalantly against the breakfast bar. "Tell me about that woman who was here yesterday."

"Do you mean Rebekah?" she asked, even though she already knew the answer was yes. If Jack had been interested in Lyda, surely he would have stayed and made a mask, even though he was already wearing one.

He nodded. "Blonde hair, blue eyes, clipboard…"

Of course he meant Rebekah. "All you need to know about her is that she's engaged to a wonderful man she is deeply in love with."

"And by that you mean some old, rich farmer who's about to kick the bucket and leave the bulk of his wealth to her?" he said dryly.

That had escalated quickly. This man apparently did not handle rejection well, and it hadn't even come from the woman herself. "Try 'thirty-year-old veterinarian who is in great shape, and while not exactly poor, lives in a rental outside of town while he saves up for a house.'"

"Interesting," he said after a moment. "So what then, she lives off of mommy and daddy's money while she waits on this guy to strike it rich?"

The nerve of this guy! "I'll have you know, she hasn't received a dime from her parents in almost a year and has worked her tail off to build a successful business all on her own!"

"Oh yeah? Doing what?"

"Not that it's any of your business, but she's an event planner, hence the clipboard you saw her with yesterday." Grace stopped just short of saying 'duh'. It was obvious she had spent too much time with Shelley, though if ever there was someone who deserved that kind of attitude, it was this guy. Speaking of Shelley... "Why do you care about Rebekah anyway? I thought you were into Shelley?"

"Who's Shelley?" he asked.

It was hard to tell since the top half of his face was covered, but she was pretty certain he was serious. "The woman in the wedding dress," Grace explained. "The one you were chasing around the carnival the other day. Do either of those ring a bell?"

"I have no idea what you're talking about," he said, his voice dripping with disdain. "I haven't chased anyone, nor would I."

Did that mean there were two men running around town in Mardi Gras masks? Or was Jack lying? For once, she would love to talk to Shelley about this, but since she was still on the warpath, that option was not on the table—if Shelley could even be counted on to tell the truth in the first place.

"You don't like me very much, do you?" he asked bluntly, catching her off guard.

Grace opened her mouth to speak, then shut it again. This man was one of her guests, so offending him was not wise—not that she hadn't already done that a million times over in just this conversation alone. "Most of my guests come here to celebrate the holiday," she said diplomatically. "You, on the other hand, seem to be here for an entirely different reason, one I am not privy to, and that makes me nervous. It also makes it difficult to provide the level of service I'm used to providing, and that causes me anxiety," she said honestly.

The part of his face she could see appeared to soften. "I'm not your enemy, Grace."

"Then what are you?"

"A man on a very personal and important mission." He turned on his heel and left, leaving her in stunned silence.

She watched him go, unsure of where she was supposed to go from there. Despite her reservations, there was a part of her that believed him. She just hoped that it wouldn't come back to bite her later.

***

"Hey strangers!" Grace said as she joined Carl, Katherine, Granny, Julian, Gladys, and Earl. They were seated on the sidewalk in the back of the crowd that had gathered for the concert. "I feel like I haven't seen you guys in ages!" She bent down and gave them each a hug, breathing in the scent of cinnamon and sugar that still clung to their clothes.

Carl patted a chair next to him. "Come sit down," he offered. "We've got another chair for that hubby of yours if he shows up."

Grateful for the opportunity to rest, Grace took him up on his offer. She'd been running around all day. If she wasn't cleaning, she was cooking, and if she wasn't cooking, she was helping to put out fires all over town. Who knew hosting these events could be so much work!

"So," Grace said, leaning forward so she could see them all. "How was your job as bakery assistants? Have you had enough fun, or should I watch out for an invitation to the grand opening of your new bakery back home?"

Katherine exchanged a look with Carl, then smiled. "I don't know about this one, but I think I've had my fill of work for a while. At this point, I need a vacation from my vacation!"

Guilt slapped Grace in the face so hard she almost fell out of her chair. "I am so sorry, you guys. I—"

"Hush," Carl interrupted. "No one forced us to do it, we volunteered. Besides that, we had a good time, didn't we, Katherine?"

"Oh yes," she nodded. "It was certainly an experience I'll never forget!"

Grace was pretty sure that was a nice way of saying she hated every second of it. Not that she blamed her. She'd be perfectly fine to never work in a bakery again!

"What about you two?" Grace asked Granny and Gladys. "Will you be picking up any more shifts at the bakery?"

"We might pick up a few around the holidays," Granny mused. "If Jilly still needs us..."

That sounded ominous. She was almost afraid to ask, but was dying to know, so she decided to risk it. "Did Jilly and Jenny get along alright?"

The four of them shifted uncomfortably, their gazes anywhere but on her.

"Let's just say they survived the week," Gladys said diplomatically.

So much for her hope the two of them would make amends. She considered talking to them again, but figured at this point she'd meddled enough. Did that mean she was making progress on her goal to stop interfering in everyone else's lives? She certainly hoped so.

"What band is playing tonight?" Carl asked, his attention now on the stage where the musicians were setting up.

"Oh! You're going to love them!" Grace said enthusiastically. "Somehow, Rebekah managed to book a local country band. They're not 'world famous,' but they are a big enough name that they play at the state fair every year!"

Speaking of Rebekah, Grace watched her friend make a mad dash through the crowd, Jack right behind her. Her goal to give up meddling was now out the window as she chased after them. When she finally caught up, they were inside town hall, Katie's former desk separating them.

"What's going on in here?" Grace asked, immediately going to Rebekah's side. She pulled out her phone and held it up for Jack to see. "Should I call the police?"

Jack held up his hands and took a couple of steps back. "No need for that, we were just talking."

"You were 'just talking,'" Rebekah accused. "I was trying to get away from you, but you refuse to leave me alone."

Grace glared at Jack. "Didn't I just tell you this morning she isn't available? And even if she wasn't engaged to a tall, muscular, martial arts expert, that still doesn't give you the right to harass her!"

Rebekah looked at Grace and raised a brow. "You're laying it on a bit thick, don't you think?"

"I'm not trying to date her!" Jack exclaimed. "Sheesh, can't a man talk to a woman without it turning into something romantic?"

"Are you trying to claim that a man visiting from New York, who plans to leave in a few days, is trying to make friends with some random woman who happens to live in the small town he's visiting? Because that makes zero sense," Grace pointed out. "And no, I don't believe that, and I doubt anyone else would either."

His mouth opened and closed a few times before he threw his hands up in frustration. "I have my reasons, okay?"

"You know what, I've had enough of this!" Rebekah yelled. She stormed over to Jack and yanked the mask off his face, then stared up at him, her eyes widening in horror. "Jackson?"

He yanked the mask back, tossed it to the ground, then stomped on it for good measure. "This was *not* how things were supposed to go," he muttered as he turned and left the building.

It took Grace a minute to connect the dots. Rebekah had only mentioned that name once in the entire time she had known her. But when she finally did, she too was left horrified. "Was that—"

"—my brother?" she finished. "Yes, it was. But... *why* is he here? And why is he hiding his identity behind that stupid mask while asking me a thousand questions?"

Grace didn't have an answer, but she knew someone who might: Molly. But the last thing she wanted to do was start drama between her two best friends, so she decided it would be best to speak to Molly in private first, and pray she had answers that wouldn't leave Rebekah feeling betrayed.

"Hey you two," Carl called out, his head poking through the door. "Mayor Allen needs you on the stage."

"Why?" Grace couldn't help but ask. She wasn't in charge of the concert; she was just an attendee like everyone else.

Carl shrugged. "I have no idea, but they're waiting to start the concert until you get there, so you'd best skedaddle before the crowd starts getting antsy."

They followed him back to the concert area, the crowd parting to form a path for them to walk through. When they got close enough to the stage to see, they saw there was a small group of people already up there waiting.

"Um, what's going on?" Grace asked Rebekah.

Cole, Granny, Julian, Thorne, and Shelley were standing in a line behind Mayor Allen, who appeared to be doing his best to entertain the crowd. When he saw Grace and Rebekah, he sighed with relief.

"Ah, now that everyone is here, it's time for the big announcement!" Mayor Allen exclaimed. He held up an envelope and waved it around. "I want to thank all of you who voted for our first ever Winterwood Mardi Gras King and Queen! I'm sure whoever won will do an amazing job representing our town!"

Grace walked over to Cole and took his hand, only half-listening to what Mayor Allen was saying. She had no idea what he meant by 'representing the town.' It's not like the winners would go on some sort of publicity tour, but she supposed it sounded better that way.

"Can I get a drumroll, please!" he asked the drummer.

Rat-a-tat-a-tat

Mayor Allen opened the envelope, pulled out the slip of paper, then smiled. "And the winners are: Cole and Grace Reed!"

"WHAT!!" Shelley shrieked. She marched over to the microphone and snatched it out of Allen's hand. "HOW DARE YOU PICK HER, SHE DIDN'T EVEN CAMPAIGN!"

Jake and Riley appeared, each hooking one arm through hers, and began to drag her off stage.

"THIS ISN'T OVER!" she screamed.

Grace hid her face against Cole's arm. She could not remember a single time in her entire life she had felt more embarrassed than she did at this moment. If Cole hadn't been squeezing her hand, and effectively keeping her in place, she would have run off into the night. In that way, Shelley was lucky. She caused the embarrassment and got to leave. Sometimes life just wasn't fair.

Mayor Allen cleared his throat, then pasted a smile on his face. "This was a close race, y'all! There were at least a dozen candidates, and while Cole and Grace were the clear winners, I'd like to give honorable mention to Julian Murray and Josephine Parker, who were a close second!"

The audience hooted and hollered as Granny and Julian waved to the crowd.

"I'd also like to congratulate Thorne Walker and Rebekah Rutherford for coming in third!"

Rebekah and Thorne, who had been standing off to the side, waved to the crowd, their faces a mixture of awe and bewilderment.

"It warms my heart to see how welcoming this town is to our newcomers," Mayor Allen continued. "Although, by this point, I think it's safe to say they are both officially one of us!"

Grace's heart swelled with emotion, her embarrassment a thing of the past. Tears stung her eyes as she watched her friends bask in the glow of the cheering crowd.

"Now, back to our King and Queen!"

Cole tugged Grace forward to stand next to the mayor, then removed his hat and bent down so Allen could place the crown on his head. Grace accepted her tiara, though she didn't have to bend to do so. To her surprise, the crowns looked amazing, and she just knew they had Lyda written all over them. Now she definitely needed to get a mask from her; the one Grace had made paled in comparison.

When Cole nudged her with his elbow, she snapped back to the present, remembering to smile and wave to the people who had so kindly voted for her. Tears stung her eyes for the second time, and she really wished she had that mask right about now.

Thankfully, Mayor Allen handed the microphone to Rebekah, which was their cue to exit the stage so she could introduce the band. Grace admired how calm and poised her friend appeared after everything that had just happened. When she grew up, she wanted to be just like her!

Cole and Grace followed Granny and Julian back to their seats, pausing every few seconds to hug and thank the people congratulating them along the way. When they finally reached the others, they hugged them too, then finally sat down.

"Would it be bad if we went home early?" Grace whispered in Cole's ear.

He gave her an assessing look, then shook his head. "Let's stay for at least one song, then we'll slip out the back, okay?"

She nodded, then leaned over and rested her head against his shoulder, the exhaustion of the day threatening to claim her right then and there. As she watched the townspeople dance and sing along to the music in front of her, she allowed herself to get lost in the music. There were still problems to solve, but they could wait—tomorrow was another day.

Days till Mardi Gras

-Four-

Jack did not come down to breakfast, nor did he answer his door when Grace knocked on it. She didn't think he'd left, but she wouldn't know for sure until she cleaned his room later that morning. It was hard to fathom what game he was playing, but his questions about Rebekah now made a lot more sense. So did his accusations. She hadn't picked up on it at first, but his belief Rebekah was living off her parents' money was a pretty bold assumption. That simply wasn't something you went around accusing strangers of doing.

Unfortunately, Rebekah had gone silent as well. Grace had tried to call and text her multiple times, but so far, all of her messages had been left on read. If she didn't surface soon, Grace would have to track her down.

Since the carnival was now over, she was back to providing entertainment for the guests. Today was the 5K bead run, but that wasn't until the afternoon, which meant she needed to give them something to do in the meantime. Luckily for her, they'd all thought it would be fun to spend the morning hanging out at Brynn's coffee shop. A local author had jumped at the chance to give a talk on one of their books, and to her surprise, even Eva had seemed excited about it. Honestly, she was a little jealous. A relaxing morning at the coffee shop sounded like heaven right about now.

Grace had just finished wiping down the dining room table when Molly walked in.

"Did you hear the news?" she asked, tapping her foot impatiently. When Grace gave her a blank look and went back to cleaning, Molly huffed out a breath and grabbed the sponge, tossing it in the sink like it was a basketball in a hoop. "Mayor Allen has called an emergency town council meeting," she announced, grabbing Grace's hand and yanking her toward the door. "And we need to get there now!"

"What's the rush?" Grace asked, yanking her hand free so she could grab her coat and purse. "They can't wait five minutes?"

"Not this time."

They jogged to Molly's waiting car, which she had left running at the curb. When they reached the town hall, Molly parked at her office across the street, then rushed to the meeting room, Grace right behind her.

Despite Molly's insistence they couldn't be late, they were the first ones there. Not even Mayor Allen was present, though Grace assumed he was in his office.

"Sooo, since it seems like we'll be waiting a bit for everyone to show up, why don't we talk about Jack?" Grace suggested. "Or should I say, *Jackson*?"

Molly's head whipped toward Grace so fast it almost startled her out of her chair.

"Does Rebekah know?"

Grace nodded. "But only that her brother is in town. She has no idea you knew and hid it from her. Yet."

"Are you going to tell her?"

"No, I'm not," Grace replied. "Because you're going to. Why did you do it, Molly? Rebekah is your friend. Why would you betray her for some stranger you've never met before?"

"Would you accept that there are still things you don't know?"

Several members of the council walked in, their chatter loud and boisterous.

"No, I won't," Grace said quietly. "And neither will Rebekah. Not this time."

More people filed in and took their seats, Rebekah among them. When she saw Grace, she took a seat beside her.

"Sorry," she whispered. "I've been with Jackson all morning. I'll tell you about it later."

Once everyone had arrived and was seated, Mayor Allen entered the room and took his spot behind the podium, his expression somber.

"It is with a heavy heart that I must inform you that Katie, our town manager, has been caught embezzling money from the town coffers."

Gasps rang out around the room as council members began whispering amongst themselves.

"What's going to happen to her?" Addie asked.

He hesitated before responding, the words difficult to say out loud. "Prosecutors are currently working out the terms of a plea deal, but some jail time is guaranteed."

Even though Grace had already heard the news, it was still difficult to hear it again. With Riley, there had still been hope Katie was innocent and this was all a big misunderstanding. Now, it seemed all hope was gone.

"Who's going to replace her?" Lyda asked, ever the pragmatic one.

The door burst open as Shelley came bounding in. She was dressed in a white silk dress, the train of which was at least six feet long. "It should be me!" she exclaimed, her thumb hiked toward her chest. "My family has been a part of this town for decades! If anyone deserves this, I do!"

Grace knew Shelley was talking about the title of Mardi Gras Queen. It quickly became apparent her fellow council members thought she was talking about the manager position.

"I don't see why we shouldn't give her a chance," Mr. Wilkins said. "What's the worst that could happen?"

Was he serious? The worst had just happened, and that was with someone who wasn't a self-absorbed drama queen.

"Wait!" Grace interjected. "That's not what she's—"

"Let him talk," Shelley interrupted with a smirk.

"You guys cannot be serious," Grace said. She crossed her arms and slumped down in her chair.

Addie turned to her and gave her a stern look. "Now Grace, don't be a poor sport. Everyone deserves a second chance."

In that case, they might as well give Katie back her job. Did they really think Shelley—who had zero office skills—could run the town? And why wasn't Mayor Allen objecting? Was Grace the only one there who hadn't lost their mind?

"But—"

"Yeah, Grace, don't be such a poor sport," Shelley snarked.

"Alright, fine," Grace said. "If this is what the council wants, so be it."

Shelley jumped up and down, her hands clapping in glee. "Eeeee, you won't regret this!" She stuck her tongue out at Grace, then turned and left, her fist pumping in the air as she ran.

Grace briefly considered volunteering to be the one to tell Shelley she now had a job. It would almost be worth it to see the look on her face when Shelley learned not only was she still not the queen, she was expected to actually work. But no, she was going to leave that bit of fun to one of Shelley's 'supporters.' Far be it from her to deny them the privilege of witnessing one of Shelley's tantrums in all its drama-filled glory.

Since she had no desire to support this nonsense, Grace got up and walked out, completely ignoring the gasps and whispers as she did so. She'd always known she would regret the day she allowed Shelley to stay, but never in her wildest dreams did she think this would be why.

***

It was almost time for the big race, and Grace reluctantly showed up for it. She'd spent the morning hiding out at the hotel, uninterested in seeing anyone from the town council, including Molly, who had been uncharacteristically silent throughout the whole Shelley debacle.

As she walked down Main Street, she was surprised to discover that most of the carnival was already packed up and ready to go. Only the really big rides were left, but even they were in the process of being dismantled and loaded onto the trailers they came on. She was sad to see it go, but relieved she was back to only cooking one breakfast each morning, not to mention only cleaning one set of rooms.

When she reached the starting line for the race, which happened to be the area where the concert had taken place the night before, she looked around for her guests, spotting them over by the stage area.

"Hey guys," Grace called out as she walked over to them. "Are you ready for some exercise!"

Eva rolled her eyes. "Exercise is a yoga session followed by a kale smoothie. This," she waved her hand toward the crowd that had gathered, "is organized chaos."

"Isn't that the best kind?" Grace joked. When Eva didn't laugh, Grace tried another tactic. "You'll get plenty of beads…"

For some reason, the promise of beads did the trick. Grace had no idea why they held so much appeal, but to each their own.

Jasmine, who had been on the ground stretching, popped up. "Are you going to run with us?" she asked Grace.

That had initially been her plan, but after the morning she'd had, she was no longer in the mood. Between Molly, Rebekah, Jackson, Shelley, and now the entire town council, she was both physically and emotionally exhausted.

"I'm going to wait here for you to come back and help crown the winner!" she said with as much enthusiasm as she could muster.

"Where exactly is the route?" Phillip asked. He had a map, but he kept rotating it, clearly lost.

Grace pointed up Main Street. "You're going to go straight up this street, past the B&B, and down to the high school. Once you get there, you'll turn around and run right back here, where I'll be waiting."

Mayor Allen approached the starting line, a megaphone raised to his lips. "Can I have your attention, please," his voice blared. "It's almost time to start the race. Please take your positions!"

"Good luck, everyone!" Grace called out as they left to take their places. She looked around for Carl and Katherine, then remembered they had volunteered to toss out beads along the route.

Bang

He fired the shot to start the race, then hopped out of the way as runners flew past him and up the street.

Seconds later, Grace and Mayor Allen were alone.

"Why didn't you stop that foolishness this morning?" Grace asked, her voice full of accusation. "You know darn well Shelley is not a candidate for the town manager position."

"Sometimes the best way to teach people a lesson is to let them see the error of their ways," he replied.

"Meaning?" Grace asked, in no mood to decipher his cryptic reply.

Mayor Allen wrapped his arm around her shoulder and led her over to a nearby bench. "Meaning I tasked Addie and Mr. Wilkins with telling Shelley the good news," he said with a laugh.

So they'd had the same thought all along. "You are devious," Grace told him, a grin spreading across her lips. "The only thing that would have been better is if you made them record it so we could watch it later!"

"The thought may have crossed my mind, but I figured that might be taking things a wee bit too far," he said, holding his thumb and pointer finger close together.

As they waited for the first of the runners to return, Rebekah showed up, a bag of ribbons in hand.

"Next time you decide to walk out of a meeting, you better take me with you," she said to Grace.

"No one stopped you from following me," Grace shot back.

Rebekah shrugged. "I was so stunned I don't think I moved a muscle for a solid five minutes."

"To be fair, I don't think anyone else did either," Allen quipped.

Part of her felt good to have that kind of power. The other part was a little ashamed by her unprofessional behavior. Then again, how else was she supposed to convey her feelings to people who refused to listen? Sometimes actions spoke louder than words.

"Are you ready to tell me about your brother?" Grace asked. She felt guilty for bringing it up in front of Mayor Allen, but she couldn't stand the suspense any longer.

Rebekah sighed and took a seat next to Grace. "Apparently our mom has been trying to convince him to go home, and one of the ways she's done that is by promising him we've changed."

"By 'we' I assume she means you?" Grace drawled.

"She certainly didn't mean her and my dad," Rebekah snapped. She winced, then shook her head. "I'm sorry, it's just so like them to lie and manipulate people to their advantage. Even my brother thinks his behavior is justified, and he's supposed to be the 'enlightened' one."

"I'm still not sure I understand," Grace told her. "Did he come here to spy on you?"

Mayor Allen cleared his throat. "I don't mean to interrupt, but it looks like our first runner is just about to cross the finish line."

Grace and Rebekah stood and took their places, each with a ribbon in hand.

"That's exactly what he was doing," Rebekah continued as they waited. "When he wasn't stalking me, he was grilling all my friends. It's pretty humiliating when you think about it."

It was a pretty scummy thing to do, but Grace had already figured that part out, so she wasn't surprised. She just wished she had figured it out sooner. But who would have ever guessed something like this could happen?

Things began to happen so fast they ran together in a blur. One by one, and sometimes three by three, people began to cross the finish line. Grace had never smiled and clapped this much in her life. When her guests made their way back, she clapped even harder, whooping and cheering to make them feel special.

"You guys did great!" Grace called out to them. "Looks like you could open a bead store if you went in together," she teased, admiring all the colorful necklaces they were sporting. "Did you have fun?"

"It was awesome!" Jasmine said, high-fiving Dwayne. "We need to do more of these when we get back home."

Dwayne groaned. "Thanks a lot, Grace, you've created a monster!"

"That's actually not a bad idea," Eva said. "It will help you work off all those donuts."

"Oh no," Dwayne moaned, covering his face with his hands. "Now there's two of them making donut jokes!"

Eva nudged Jasmine with her elbow. "Race you back to the B&B. Winner gets the last piece of king cake!"

"You are so on!"

They took off, their husbands trailing behind them at a much slower pace.

"Guess they had a good time," Rebekah said, watching as they playfully pushed each other as they ran.

"I am honestly shocked to see them getting along so well," Grace replied. "Maybe Eva has become somewhat 'enchanted' after all."

A few of the stragglers wandered in, the crowd clapping and cheering them across the finish line. As events went, Grace considered this one a success. She too will have to do some more of these in the future.

Once all the ribbons had been handed out, Grace and Rebekah linked arms and began the walk down to the B&B.

"You never finished telling me about Jackson," Grace reminded her. "Is he still here? Or has he taken off for parts unknown?"

"As far as I know, he's still here, but I'm not sure he would tell me if he left."

"How did you leave things? Does he believe that you've 'changed?'" Grace asked, certain that must be the case. No way Jackson was unable to see the difference between the old Rebekah and the woman she is now.

Rebekah was silent for a few minutes. "Honestly, I have no idea what he believes. I was so angry with him for doing that to me, I refused to listen to a word he had to say. So we're no better off now than we were ten years ago when I went to see him at the commune."

She sounded so sad, Grace's heart ached for her. Somehow, she would fix this. Never mind her goal to stop meddling. That could wait until after her friend's crisis had been solved.

Days till Mardi Gras

-Three-

Grace walked into the dining room, halting abruptly when she saw Jackson seated at the table as if nothing had happened. "Okay everyone!" she said as she took her seat at the table, side-eyeing him as she made her announcement. "This afternoon is the parade, but since tomorrow is the Cajun cook-off, I thought you might want to spend the morning practicing your recipes."

Jasmine eyed the kitchen, then the people at the table. "No offense, Grace, but I don't think we'll all fit in there, and I'm not willing to risk a finger to try."

It was a little offensive they thought she'd risk their health—what kind of host did they think she was? But she could see their point. Luckily, she already had a solution. "I plan to take you over to the hotel to cook," Grace explained. "It has a large, commercial kitchen that could easily accommodate everyone here without risking a finger!"

"Where's that husband of yours?" Jackson asked. Now that his identity had been exposed, he no longer wore the mask. "We never see him at breakfast, and since today is a Saturday, you can't claim work as an excuse." He leaned back in his chair, his hands crossed behind his head, a smirk on his face turning it from handsome to malevolent.

"I've been curious about that, too," Eva said. "Not that it matters, it just seems strange he's never around."

Jackson let out a derisive laugh. "He's probably down at the pond fishing and drinking beer with his buddies while the missus here does all the work. Isn't that how y'all do things around here?" he said in an exaggerated southern accent.

Grace attempted to swallow her anger, then changed her mind. Why should she be the only one at the table with any decorum? "I'll have you know, my husband is a farmer," she spit out. "He gets up at five in the morning every morning so that people like you have food to eat. Both he and every other farmer in the world deserve nothing but the utmost respect from people like you!"

His chair plopped forward with a thud, his smirk gone. "I—"

"I'm not done," Grace said, cutting him off. "For someone who is supposed to have spent the last fifteen or so years living at a commune, you are awfully rude and judgmental. Where is all that 'love and peace' you're supposed to have preached?" She shook her head in disgust. "Your sister has changed, Jackson, but it is clear you have not. Go back to New York. I have a feeling it will be as if you never left."

In lieu of an actual microphone to drop, Grace had to be content with shoving back her chair and storming out of the room. She made it to the foyer when she remembered she still had to deal with the rest of her guests.

"Those of you who want to go to the hotel," she said as she popped her head back in the room, "be ready to go in twenty." She paused in the foyer again, taking a moment to calm down as she leaned against the railing. When she was confident she could speak without anger, she returned to the dining room a third time.

"I apologize to everyone but Jackson," she said, startling a laugh out of them. "While I do not tolerate disrespect in this house, I have no desire to make anyone uncomfortable either, nor should I have discussed personal information in front of the group. For that, I do apologize to Jackson." She paused to look at him, then turned her attention back to the others. "As I said, be ready to go in twenty minutes."

This time when she left, she went to her room, anxious to have a few minutes to herself to reflect. She had been right in everything she said, yet her delivery could have been better. Telling Jackson off had felt good in the moment, but it was not worth the potential damage she did to her reputation in front of the others.

Knock Knock

Assuming it was Eva or Jasmine, Grace took a deep breath, then opened the door—only it wasn't one of them.

"I owe you an apology," Jackson told her, his head lowered in contrition. "There are at least a dozen excuses I could make for my behavior, but that's all they'd be—excuses. So, I hope you'll accept my sincere apology instead."

This was completely unexpected, and she wasn't sure how to respond. While she hadn't liked his comments about Cole, she was hardly the victim here. "I appreciate that," she said. "But I think Rebekah is the one who deserves the apology. She's an amazing person who's worked really hard to build a new life for herself without the support of her parents. If you got to know who she is now, you would see she's someone to be proud of."

Jackson nodded. "That's what Mom said, but I guess I just couldn't reconcile that with the teenager who came to see me a decade ago. Worse than that, it seems the second I stepped back into my family's orbit, I fell right back into my old habits." He ran a hand down his face, then shook his head. "Honestly, Grace, that's why I left in the first place. I hate who I become when I'm 'Jackson Rutherford.'"

It was times like this she wished she had someone else's advice to channel. What do you say to someone in a situation like this? "I wish I could say I understand, but I don't. I've always just been me, flaws and all. Maybe what you need is to accept who you are. Trying to run from part of yourself sounds exhausting."

He appeared to think about that. "I think you're right," he said. "Thanks, Grace."

She was about to close the door when it dawned on her what he'd said. "Wait a minute, did you say Jackie told you Rebekah was someone to be proud of?"

Jackson turned around and smiled. "I was stunned too. I don't know what kind of magic you're casting here, but whatever it is, it's working!"

This time, when he turned to leave, she let him. She closed the door and leaned against it in stunned silence. Imagine that—Jacqueline Rutherford, of all people, was proud of her wayward daughter. Maybe she should have named this place the Miracle Inn after all.

***

Grace had just gotten back from the hotel, and what she considered to be a successful practice run for tomorrow, when Rebekah and Lyda showed up.

"You're not ready," Rebekah said, frowning at Grace's jeans and sweater.

"Ready for what?" Grace asked as she gave herself a quick once-over. As far as she could tell, there was nothing wrong with what she was wearing. Sure, her sweater was a little stained from accidentally splashing some dirty water on it while doing the dishes, but so what? All she had planned for the rest of the day was dinner and the parade. Who cared if she stood in her yard with a dirty shirt? She'd be wearing a jacket anyway.

Lyda set the box she was holding down on the table and pulled out a mask, which she then handed to Grace. "I need to see if this goes well with your tiara," she told Grace. "What color is the dress you're wearing? Purple? Green? Gold?"

An anxious feeling began to form in the bottom of Grace's stomach. "You're talking about the dress for the masquerade ball, right?"

Rebekah stared at Grace in horror. "She's talking about the dress you're supposed to be wearing for the parade!

You're the Mardi Gras Queen, remember? You and Cole are supposed to ride on the main parade float. Like Santa in the Macy's Thanksgiving Day Parade!"

Grace looked from Lyda to Rebekah, unable to comprehend what she was hearing. Why had no one told her this before? Probably because it had been her idea—only she had expected someone else, ANYONE else, to be queen. What was she supposed to do now? "Can I wear the same dress I planned to wear to the ball?" she asked, her tone pleading. "It's black, but that means it will go with anything, right?"

Lyda rolled her eyes. "You can NOT wear black to one of the most colorful events in the world! You will stick out like a sore thumb! Besides that, people might get the wrong idea and think you're equating it to a funeral or something."

"Think Shelley will let me borrow one of her wedding dresses?" Grace joked.

When they crossed their arms and gave her 'the look,' she knew she was in trouble.

"Okay, fine, what am I supposed to do? The fanciest dress I own is my wedding dress, and I haven't picked that up from the cleaners yet." A terrible thought crossed her mind. "Does Cole know about this?" Of course he doesn't, because the one who would have told him is her. She felt like she could pass out. How had she managed to screw up her own event this badly?

Rebekah walked over and pushed Grace into a chair. "Breathe," she commanded. She picked up her clipboard and began to fan Grace, then turned to Lyda. "She could always wear the silver dress I wore for her wedding. It's a little too long for her, but as long as she doesn't move around too much, it should be fine."

"I don't know," Lyda replied, her lips pursed. "The silver would clash with the gold. I have plenty of colorful dresses, but I'm afraid she'll have the opposite problem and they'll be too short."

Granny appeared in the doorway, took one look at them, then pulled out a chair and sat down. "What crisis are we solving today?" she quipped.

"Grace needs a dress to wear to the parade," Rebekah explained. "And somehow, she failed to get one."

"You know I'm sitting right here," Grace said sulkily. "And what about Cole? What is he supposed to do?"

Rebekah cocked her head. "He actually could wear the same thing he wore to the wedding."

Lyda nodded in agreement. "Someone, *ahem*," she said, loudly clearing her throat, "should probably let him know so he can get ready."

Men really did have it easy. All they needed was one good suit, and that would carry them through their entire lives. Why couldn't women do that too?

"Earth to Grace," Rebekah called out as she snapped her fingers. When Grace looked up at her, Rebekah handed her the phone. "You need to call Cole," she reminded her.

Grace accepted the phone, then pulled up Cole's number and hit the call button. As she waited for him to answer, she studied his picture, tracing the outline of his face with her pointer finger. He really was a handsome man, especially the way his dimples showed when he smiled. She was really lucky she found him. So lucky...

"Hello? Grace?" Cole repeated her name a few times before she snapped out of it.

"Hi!" she finally said, snapping out of her reverie. She explained the situation, then let out a sigh of relief when he said he'd be there soon. One problem down, one to go. If only hers could be solved so easily. Grace looked up at Lyda and narrowed her eyes. "It's cold out there," she pointed out. "Do I really have to wear a dress? I'm going to freeze to death!"

"I'll let you wear a coat," Lyda compromised. She turned her attention to Granny. "What about that green sequinned dress you bought at New Year's? Do you think Grace could borrow that?"

Granny nodded, then left to fetch the dress. She returned a few minutes later, holding it up so they could examine it.

"That's perfect!" Rebekah exclaimed. She picked up the mask and held it up to the dress. "It's so perfect you would think we planned it!"

Grace accepted the dress, then walked toward the foyer. "I'm wearing leggings underneath this," she called over her shoulder. "And you can't stop me!"

By the time Grace returned to the dining room, Cole had arrived, looking more handsome than ever in his suit. His face lit up when he saw her in Granny's dress.

"There's my Queen!" he said as he took her hand and twirled her around in a circle. "You look beautiful!"

"You both look amazing," Rebekah said as she handed them their crowns. "But we need to go or you're going to be late."

Once their crowns were in place, Lyda handed them their masks, then stepped back to assess her work. "Try to be careful, I only have enough supplies left for very minor repairs," she warned them.

It was difficult to see through the mask, so Grace took Cole's hand and allowed him to lead her to his truck. Surprisingly, she wasn't even cold despite the below-freezing temperatures. Maybe this wouldn't be so bad after all.

When they arrived at the high school, Grace lowered her mask to see the finished parade floats. Even though she'd had zero doubts the design committee would come through with something amazing, she was still blown away by the creativity of those involved. In her completely unbiased opinion, these floats could easily slip right into a New Orleans Mardi Gras parade, and no one would be the wiser.

Hopefully someone would take pictures. She should call Carl and ask him to take some for her. While she waited to be told where to go, she did just that, unsurprised to hear he already had his camera out and was ready to go.

"Okay you two," Rebekah called out as she waved them over to the last float in line. "You're going to stand in the middle of those X's. There's at least a dozen bags of beads for you to toss to the crowd, but you have a long way to go, so try to conserve some for the end of the parade, okay?"

Cole helped Grace onto the float, then wrapped a steadying arm around her shoulder. When it was their turn to move, the trailer lurched forward, Grace and Cole with it. Somehow, he managed to keep them upright despite her clinging tightly to him.

"I'm not letting go," Grace told him.

He chuckled, his lips grazing her ear. "It's okay, you just need a minute to get used to it, that's all."

They managed to make it out of the parking lot without further incident, but as promised, Grace kept close to him just in case. Once they were on the street, she heard shouting behind her and turned to see Shelley sitting on top of the trunk in the back of a convertible, a massive crown on her head, a Mardi Gras Queen sash firmly in place across another of her wedding dresses. Where she kept finding those was still a mystery.

More curious than that was the man driving the car. He was wearing the same Mardi Gras mask Jackson had been wearing. Surely it wasn't him, right?

Rebekah and a few of the other volunteers chased after them, but it quickly became clear Shelley had zero intention of listening to them, and there was nothing they could do about it. To her credit, Rebekah at least tore the sign that read, 'True Mardi Gras Queen,' off the side of the car and ripped it up as Shelley screeched in protest. As things went, if this was the worst Shelley had planned, it was pretty tame. But that was a big IF. There was still the ball...

They continued down the street, Grace doing her best to ignore Shelley's persistent yelling that she was the 'true queen,' while Grace waved and tossed beads to the people lined up on the side. When they reached the B&B, she waved enthusiastically to her guests, surprised to see that Jackson was among them. If he isn't the one driving Shelley's car, then who is? Somehow, she needed to get to the bottom of this mystery, the sooner the better.

Days till Mardi Gras

-Two-

I t was still dark out when Grace woke up. Some habits were hard to break, even when she felt like she could still sleep for at least another few hours. She could tell from the sound of his breathing that Cole was asleep, so she slid across the bed and snuggled up against him. When his arm wrapped around her and pulled her close, she looked up at his face in surprise.

"How long have you been awake?"

"Since about the time someone put their ice-cold feet up against my legs," he drawled.

"Sorry," Grace whispered as she moved her feet. "I think I kicked my socks off in the middle of the night by accident." She lay there for a moment, then raised up on her elbow so she could see him better. "Things have been so crazy, I keep forgetting to ask how Riley is doing."

He scrunched his nose. "He's been taking the news of Katie's guilt pretty hard. Apparently, she claims she did it for them and their future. Now there's no them, and no future..."

Her heart ached for Riley. She couldn't imagine how hard it must be to find out the person you love was guilty of a crime like that.

"He's not leaving," Cole informed her. "He offered to, but I told him we wanted him to stay and would give him our full support."

"Of course we will," Grace said absentmindedly. Her mind was already going through the list of single women in town before she realized how insensitive that might seem, given the circumstances. At the very least, he could be Lyda's date for the ball. Nothing wrong with two friends spending the evening together...

Cole reached up and tilted her face down toward his. "Whatever it is you're planning, please don't."

"Why does everyone keep saying that to me?" she asked as she batted her eyelashes at him. "I am completely innocent, I swear!"

"Mmmhmm." He pulled her back to his chest and hugged her close.

"I miss being home," Grace said softly. She still loved it here—that would never change—but she missed the coziness of the farmhouse. She also missed her fur-babies. At least Cole was here with her. If she'd had to leave him behind too, it would have been unbearable.

Cole kissed the top of her head. "I do too, darlin', but we're only here for a few more days."

Beep Beep Beep

"Already?" Grace muttered as she rolled over to turn off the alarm. Why did her time with Cole always seem to pass so quickly? "Duty calls," she told him as she found her socks and put them back on. "Sorry I woke you. If you want to sleep a little more, I can come back and get you when breakfast is ready."

He got up and began to get ready. "Thanks, babe, but I can help you cook."

Grace wrapped her arms around his waist and hugged him tight. "You really are the best husband in the world!"

"Make sure you remember that the next time you're mad at me," he teased.

They went downstairs together, Cole instinctively going to the coffee maker while Grace began pulling out ingredients for omelets and hash browns. As the guests came down, Grace asked them what type of omelet they wanted, opting to serve them fresh.

Once everyone had been served and was seated at the table, Grace brought up the cook-off. "The cook-off officially begins at noon!" she announced. "So you need to have your dishes cooked and ready to serve around eleven-forty-five. If we leave here around nine, will that give everyone enough time to get ready?"

Jasmine nodded, then put her fork down and turned her whole body toward Grace. "Girl, forget about that, we need to talk about that Shelley chick and the crazy stunt she pulled yesterday!"

Grace groaned and shook her head. Clearly, her plan to avoid and ignore all things 'Shelley-related' was not working. "I will be the first to admit she's a little crazy," she said slowly. "But the more you engage with her and her nonsense, the more it seems to encourage her."

Eva snorted. "The other, and far more likely, scenario is the more you allow her to get away with her nonsense, the more emboldened she becomes."

That was a fair point, but how do you stop a grown woman who has no sense of shame? The whole reason she was there in the first place was because she snuck onto a movie set and caused so much damage she broke her own arm. If Shelley is willing to do something like that, what could Grace do to stop her?

"Morning, everyone," Shelley called out as she walked in. She was still wearing the same dress from yesterday, which now looked wrinkled and slept-in.

Jasmine eyed her up and down, her nose scrunching in disgust. "You have a lot of nerve showing up here after what you did!"

Shelley looked at her in surprise. "What did I do?" she asked innocently.

"She really thinks she didn't do anything wrong, doesn't she?" Jasmine asked Grace.

Grace wanted to shout, 'see, I told you it was no use,' but she held her tongue. "Who's the guy that drove your car yesterday?" Grace asked Shelley instead.

A mischievous look lit up Shelley's face. "Wouldn't you like to know," she said coyly.

"Yes, I would," Grace said sternly. "That's why I asked."

"Well, too bad! I'm not telling, and you can't make me!" She stuck her tongue out for good measure, then flounced out of the room, leaving them to stare after her.

"Don't say it," Grace warned Cole. "I don't even have to look at you to know you're thinking it."

Cole grabbed her hand under the table and gave it a reassuring squeeze. "I wasn't going to say a word."

Jackson grinned at them, obviously amused. "It's nice to see you this morning, Cole," he said. "I hope you're not here because of yesterday."

"What happened yesterday?" Cole asked, his brow furrowed in confusion.

"Oh, not much. I just made an off-color remark about you not being here much, and your lovely wife nearly took my head off!" Jackson laughed, clearly trying to make light of the situation.

Embarrassment colored Grace's cheeks as she flashed back to her outburst. She would never regret defending her husband, but she did regret doing it publicly. Especially since everyone was now looking at her expectantly, though why that was, she had no idea. Instead, she clapped her hands together and pushed her chair back. "We need to get moving if we're going to make it to the cook-off in time," she informed them.

Once the guests left to grab their coats and purses, Cole and Grace found themselves alone in the kitchen.

"It seems I owe my knight in shining armor a debt of gratitude," Cole teased. He backed her into a corner, his arms coming to rest on either side of her.

She looked up into his eyes, then smiled when she saw the twinkle in them. "I am humbled to defend your honor, my lord, but perhaps a token of appreciation would not be amiss..."

His right hand moved to the side of her face, gently cupping her cheek as he lowered his lips to hers. "Thank you," he whispered once they'd parted.

"Ahem," Jackson coughed. "Sorry to interrupt, but we're ready to go." He nodded toward the foyer, where everyone was waiting.

Grace kissed Cole's cheek, then whispered in his ear. "We'll finish this later." She grabbed her coat and purse, then led the way out the door. "Alright, everyone, let's go!"

***

When they reached the hotel, Granny, Gladys, Carl, and Katherine were waiting for them in the parking lot.

"Do you have room for a few more?" Granny asked.

"Of course!" Grace replied enthusiastically. She opened the door to the lobby, then held it open as everyone walked in. "I didn't know you planned to enter the competition," Grace said to Granny as they followed the group to the kitchen. "What are you making?"

"Gladys and I decided to enter a special king cake recipe we came up with while working at the bakery," Granny explained. "We figured we made enough of them, might as well give it a shot!"

Grace couldn't fault them for that. She briefly wondered if Jenny would do the same, then decided not to borrow trouble. Jilly, Addie, and Mayor Allen were doing the judging, and she did not want to think about the chaos that would ensue if Jilly had to judge Jenny's entry.

"I look forward to trying it!" Grace said enthusiastically.

While the group busied themselves with getting their stations set up, Grace handed out ingredients. Once everyone had everything they needed, she wandered off to the side, content to sit down and observe for once.

"Aren't you making something, Grace?" Jasmine asked as she liberally sprinkled a mixture of herbs and spices into a bowl.

"Oh no," Grace said, shaking her head. "It became clear a week ago this challenge is not for me!"

Jasmine laughed. "Was it that bad?"

"Yes!" Carl, Katherine, Granny, and Gladys said in unison.

"If you guys don't watch it, I'm letting Rebekah take over breakfast again!" Grace teased.

The four of them looked at each other in mock horror. "We're sorry!" they said in unison again.

"That's more like it!" Grace said as everyone laughed.

As they continued to cook, Grace decided to wander over to the ballroom and check on the progress Jim was making. Since Molly had insisted on managing the project, Grace had been cut out of the loop, which still annoyed her, but whatever.

When she reached the doors, she twisted the knob but found it was locked. "That's strange," she muttered. She pulled the keys out of her pocket and rifled through them until she found the master key. Once the door was unlocked, she tried to push it open, but it wouldn't budge.

"What on earth?" she asked out loud. She tried a few more times, to no avail. Something was blocking the door from the other side.

"Grace?" Granny called out. "Where are you?"

"I'm here!" Grace yelled back. She returned to the kitchen, where she found Granny standing in the doorway. "Did you need something?"

Granny gave her a curious look, then nodded. "We need more sugar, but we can't find it."

It was Grace's turn to give Granny a look, since the sugar was sitting on the counter right in front of them. When she pointed it out, Granny slapped her hand to her forehead.

"That's what I get for not bringing my readers!" Granny said as she laughed.

Gladys looked at Granny and rolled her eyes. "They're on your head, silly," she pointed out.

Grace laughed as Granny patted her head and grimaced when she felt her glasses. "It's okay, Granny, we all have days like this!" Granny lightly patted Grace's cheek, then went back to work, her glasses now perched on the end of her nose.

Now that everyone was back to work, Grace was tempted to go look for another way into the ballroom, then wondered why the main door was blocked in the first place. Was this Molly's doing? Was she trying to keep Grace out for some reason? Grace couldn't think of a single reason why Molly would do that, but Molly had been doing a lot of strange things as of late, so she couldn't completely rule out the idea.

Oh well, she would just have to meet Jim here tomorrow morning. Surely he would answer her questions; after all, she was the one who called him in the first place. Right?

***

The town council had decided to host the cook-off in the park, which had sounded like a good idea at the time but was now proving to be questionable. Not only was it freezing outside, the sky looked suspiciously like snow, the weather app on Grace's phone claiming a high chance for the offending 'white stuff' to make an appearance.

White tents were lined up on two opposing sides, the occupants huddled around their food warmers, drinking coffee and hot chocolate while they waited for the judges to make their rounds.

For her part, Grace had set up a large tent with an extended table long enough for everyone who wanted to participate to display their dish. There were chairs in the back, along with thermoses of coffee, tea, hot chocolate, and apple cider. She had wanted to bring a small heater, but Cole had convinced her not to, claiming the electricity it would draw might overwhelm the system and blow a circuit. That seemed unlikely to her—how many Christmas lights did they put up in the park each year?—but she obeyed and left it at home. Too bad she now regretted that decision.

"What do we have here?" Mayor Allen called out. Jilly and Addie were on either side of him, each of them with a clipboard in hand.

As the official spokesperson for the group—entrants were supposed to remain anonymous to avoid bias—Grace walked over and enthusiastically described each dish. "This first one is a King Cake," she said, handing them each a slice.

"Ooh, this tastes like a cross between a cake and a pecan pie!" Addie exclaimed. "I need this recipe when this is over!"

"Me too!" Jilly said as she took another bite. "These are better than the ones we served at the bakery!" She eyed the group behind Grace, as if trying to figure out which one was responsible.

Mayor Allen cleared his throat, then handed his plate back to Grace. "What's next?"

Grace served up three bowls, then handed one to each of them. "This is Smoked Sausage Cajun Alfredo," she told them. It smelled so good, she was tempted to serve herself a bowl, but didn't want to look like she was playing favorites. Once the judges left, she was definitely trying a little of everything.

"This is really good, too!" Jilly said as she made notes on her clipboard. "If I were at a restaurant, I'd come back for this."

Addie nodded. "I like the sausage."

"Next up is Shrimp Creole," Grace explained. "I guarantee the shrimp was properly prepared!"

The judges exchanged a look while the people behind her laughed.

"I'm starting to think I need to change up the menu at the diner," Addie mused as she finished her sample.

Mayor Allen raised a brow. "And risk the ire of your regulars?"

"It's good to ruffle the feathers of the old coots once in a while," she joked. "It's how we know they're still alive!"

"We heard that!" Granny and Gladys yelled out.

They laughed as they accepted samples of the last dish.

"Last but not least is Boudin Balls!" Grace announced. She pushed a container of remoulade, or 'creole mustard dipping sauce' for the uninitiated, over to them. "This is pork sausage made with rice and seasoning, stuffed in casing, and fried."

"Mmm," Mayor Allen said as he wiped his mouth with a napkin. "There's just something about fried food that hits different, you know?"

Jilly and Addie nodded in agreement, then made notes.

"Thanks, everyone," Mayor Allen called out with a wave.

Once they were gone, Grace turned back to the group. "I think that went well!"

She served them each a plate with a sample of all the dishes, then took one herself, savoring each bite. Maybe she should have had her guests cook after all! That thought made her realize Jackson had never made it to the hotel with the rest of them. How had she not realized that before now? Maybe he went to see Rebekah again?

They chatted while they waited, then anxiously made their way over to the 'stage area' when it was time to announce the winners.

"This was a really tough competition," Mayor Allen said. "There are no losers here, but unfortunately, we can only have a few winners." He pulled the envelope out of his pocket and removed the card. "The winner of the Best Appetizer category is: Dwayne and Jasmine Brown!"

Grace squealed in excitement as she hugged Jasmine, then watched in glee as Jasmine and Dwayne accepted their trophy. It was so exciting to have one of her guests win. She wished they all could win but knew that might raise some eyebrows if it happened.

Mayor Allen tapped the microphone a few times to get everyone's attention again. "The winner of the Best Entree category is: MaryJo Janes!"

The name was not familiar to Grace, so she looked around to see who the mystery woman was. The woman looked to be around Granny and Gladys's age, so maybe they knew her. It felt strange to live in such a small town for so long and still not know everyone.

"And now, the moment we've all been waiting for!" Mayor Allen said enthusiastically.

The audience made drum-roll noises until Mayor Allen signaled for them to stop.

"The winner of the Best Dessert category is: Josephine Parker and Gladys Mitchell!"

"WHAT!" Jenny yelled from the side of the crowd. She stormed over to the judges and pointed her finger in Jilly's face. "You rigged the competition, didn't you? You just couldn't stand to see me win! And after everything I did to help you!"

Jilly stepped back behind Mayor Allen, putting some distance between her and Jenny.

"Now look here, Jenny," Addie said sternly. "This competition was judged blind for this exact reason. ALL of the desserts we tasted were amazing, but Josie and Gladys won fair and square."

Jenny narrowed her eyes and balled her hands into fists. "I HATE you!" she yelled at Jilly. She then turned on her heel and stormed off, the crowd parting to give her space.

Grace sighed, then went to comfort Jilly. So much for the temporary truce with Jenny. Would things ever get better between them?

Days till Mardi Gras

-One-

Two more days to go and things will be back to normal, Grace thought as she got ready for the day. Of course, 'normal' still included cooking breakfast, so she supposed she wasn't off the hook on that front. At least there would be fewer people, although was that even true? For some reason, Molly, Grant, and Emilio hadn't been over since the guests had arrived. That was not normal for them, which only added to the weirdness they'd been displaying as of late. Something was going on there, and Grace had a feeling it had nothing to do with Katie or Jackson.

"HOW COULD YOU DO THIS TO ME?" Rebekah shouted so loud the entire house could hear her. "I thought you were my friend!"

Grace's eyes widened in surprise as she took off running, practically sliding down the stairs. When she reached the dining room, she found Rebekah glaring at Molly, her face flushed, her finger pointed so close to Molly's chest it was practically touching it.

"It's not what you think," Molly said helplessly.

"Oh really?" Rebekah retorted, her voice dripping with sarcasm. "Then what is it? Because from where I'm standing, it sure does look like you BETRAYED ME!"

Molly looked to Grace for help. "Please tell her it isn't like that."

If Grace had been smart, she would have stayed upstairs, out of the line of fire. But no, she just had to go rushing into danger headfirst, without a single thought to the consequences.

Before Grace could come up with a single coherent thought, Rebekah had already turned on her.

"You *knew*? And you didn't tell *me*?" Rebekah accused Grace. She threw her hands up in the air in frustration. "UGH! Out of all the people in the world, I thought for sure I could trust YOU! But no, you're just like everyone else, *aren't you*?"

"Wait! No!" Grace cried out in protest. "I didn't know about Jackson until you took his mask off," Grace explained. "The only thing I knew was that Molly had known about him the entire time, but I told her she had to tell you the truth herself. I would have never kept something like that from you!"

Panic began to rise in Grace's chest when Rebekah showed no signs of understanding. She was about to lose her best friend in the entire world, and she felt powerless to stop it.

"Grace is right," Molly said, her voice quivering. "I never told her about your brother either, just that there were things going on she wasn't aware of." She swiped at her eyes, then stiffened her back. "Can we please sit down and discuss this like adults?"

Rebekah's eyes flew open in a rage. "Are you serious? You stab me in the back and then have the AUDACITY to imply I'm not behaving like an adult? Because I think an adult would have told me the truth instead of playing...whatever game it is you're playing!" She grabbed her purse and stomped toward the door. As she passed Grace, she paused to look at her, pain evident in her eyes. "I'm not surprised by Molly's behavior. I've always known she could be ruthless. But you, on the other hand..." Tears stung her eyes as she looked away. "After everything we've been through, I just thought...you know what, never mind what I thought. What matters is that I was wrong." She stormed out of the room, then slammed the front door behind her.

Several minutes passed before either woman was able to talk, Grace recovering first.

"It wasn't enough to hurt her, you just had to drag me down with you, didn't you?" Grace accused Molly once she'd found her voice. "And for what? Some guy we don't even know?"

"For a job opportunity," Molly said quietly.

Of all the things Molly could have said, that was the last one Grace had expected. Did this mean she was about to lose two friends?

"I need to sit down," Grace said as she pulled out a chair and sank down onto it.

Molly pulled out a chair opposite her and took a seat, a defeated look on her face. "It started last Mother's

Day when Hunter's mom, Amelia, came to town," Molly began. She winced at the look on Grace's face. "I know what you're thinking, but please, let me explain. Amelia approached Grant before she left town and asked him to help her come up with an exit plan before she went home to face her husband and ask for a divorce. She didn't trust the financial advisors in New York since her husband was one of them, and, well, I'm sure I don't need to explain why that was a concern for her."

"No, I'm capable of figuring that out on my own," Grace drawled. "But what I don't understand is why you kept this from us, or what it has to do with Rebekah and Jackson."

"Grant made it a rule to never discuss his clients," Molly replied. "Their privacy is his utmost concern."

That made sense, Grace supposed. She searched her memory, but she couldn't remember a single time Grant had discussed his business with her—well, unless you counted the hotel, but she was part of that business.

"As to the second part, as you know, Amelia and Jacqueline are friends, so when Jacqueline needed help of a similar nature, Amelia recommended she talk to Grant."

"But Jackie's husband is supposed to be dying," Grace protested. "Surely she isn't trying to divorce him on his deathbed?"

Molly pursed her lips as she tried to figure out what to say. "No, she's trying to protect his company from a hostile takeover. That's why she was so ruthless in trying to force Rebekah to come home, and when that didn't work, why she began pursuing Jackson."

"I still don't see how this pertains to you and Grant."

She sighed, clearly not ready to disclose that information. "Jackson isn't here to spy on Rebekah. He's been working with Grant and Emilio and has now offered them a job working for him in New York."

Grace sat in silence, her brain unable to process the bomb Molly had just dropped on her. "Who else knows about this?"

"No one but you," Molly replied. "And I know it's a lot to ask, but I need it to stay that way until we decide what to do."

Molly and Grant were thinking about moving to New York. Of course, that meant baby Eliza would go with them. And Emilio and Vanessa. And now that Rebekah hated all of them, she would probably go too. Would Thorne go with her? How many friends was she about to lose?

Jasmine popped her head in and looked around. "Is it safe to come in?"

"Oh my gosh, I'm so sorry!" Grace said as she jumped out of her chair and raced to the kitchen. "Give me ten minutes and I'll have breakfast on the table!"

"Actually, that's what I'm here to talk about," Jasmine replied. "Eva, Phillip, Dwayne, and I are planning to spend the day in Kansas City. There's a cute bistro we want to try for breakfast, and then we plan to do some shopping!"

Grace would never admit it out loud, but her relief was instant. Now she would have time to find Rebekah and beg for her forgiveness! "Are you sure?" Grace asked, praying Jasmine said yes. "I had a scavenger hunt planned for you guys today..."

"That sounds like a ton of fun!" Jasmine said enthusiastically. "Perhaps tomorrow? Or will that interfere with the ball?"

"Tomorrow should work," Grace told her. "Have fun on your day trip!"

Jasmine waved, then returned to the foyer where the others were waiting.

Once Grace was sure they were gone, she grabbed her things. "I have to find Rebekah," she told Molly. "Are you coming?"

Molly shook her head. "I need to get back to work," she said sadly. "Please tell Rebekah I never meant to hurt her."

"You could tell her yourself," Grace pointed out. "I think it would have more impact coming from you. After all, it was your decision not to speak to her that got us in trouble in the first place."

"I wish you could understand how hard this is," Molly pleaded. "Grant and I worked so hard to build a life here together, and now..."

"And now you're about to throw it all away," Grace finished for her. "Are you sure you want to do this? You guys have already played this game once when you lived in Boston, and in case you forgot, you almost ended up divorced. You moved here to start over...had Eliza..."

Molly burst into tears. "I know," she sobbed, gratefully accepting the tissue Grace handed her. "But this is a once in a lifetime opportunity, the kind only fools pass up. How do we say no to that?"

Grace didn't have an answer for her. She would follow Cole to the edge of the world, so she didn't blame Molly one bit for supporting Grant. She just hoped when it was all said and done, what they gained was worth more than they lost.

***

Her search for Rebekah was proving fruitless. So far, Grace had checked town hall, Addie's, the bakery, Chrissy's Boutique, Brynn's coffee shop, the hotel, Thorne's house, and even the winery. It was too cold for her to be at the park, and there was no way she was at Molly's office, so where did that leave her?

It seemed unlikely Rebekah would hide out at the vet, but she went there anyway. Even if she wasn't there, if anyone would know where she was, it was Thorne.

Little bells jingled as she pushed open the door. To her delight, Thorne was standing behind the reception desk, discussing a chart with one of the vet techs. When he looked up and saw her walk in, he tried to make a run for it, but Grace raced him to his office—and won.

"She made me swear not to give you any information," Thorne said as he backed out of the room.

"Quit being such a baby and get in here!" Grace called after him. She rolled her eyes when he came back in and closed the door. "I did not betray her, but I can't convince her of that unless I'm able to talk to her."

Thorne sat down behind his desk, a defeated look on his face. "I want to help you, but I can't. I'm sorry."

There had to be a way Thorne could help without breaking his promise to Rebekah. "If you can't tell me where she is," Grace mused, "can you give me an idea of where she's going to be?"

He appeared to consider that. "A client of hers passed away," he finally replied. "That's all I can say."

Grace thought back to one of the first conversations she had with Rebekah since she'd been home and remembered her talking about the woman who had planned her own funeral. It had never occurred to her to check the funeral home, but it made sense in a weird sort of way. "Thanks, Thorne, you're the best!"

Five minutes later, she pulled into the parking lot of William and Sons Funeral Home, and sure enough, Rebekah's car was parked off to the side. Grace rushed inside and found Rebekah standing in the coffin room.

"I hope you're not imagining me in there," Grace joked as she gestured toward the nearest casket.

Rebekah gave her a scathing look. "It would serve you right if I was."

Apparently, time had not improved Rebekah's mood—it had made it worse.

"I'm sorry I didn't tell you Molly knew who Jackson was, but I really thought the news should come from her," Grace explained. "If it helps, her intent wasn't malicious, just misguided."

"Of course you would defend her," Rebekah snarked. "What's that saying? Birds of a feather flock together?"

Shades of the 'old' Rebekah were surfacing, and Grace was starting to get the feeling Jackson wasn't the only one who struggled with his Rutherford side.

"I guess I deserved that," Grace said patiently. "But I feel like there's more going on here than you just being mad about the Molly situation."

Rebekah turned to face her, tears streaming down her cheeks. "I really wanted to believe I belonged here. That I'd finally found a family that cared about me. But twice now that has proven not to be true. First, when Molly chose my brother over me. Second, when you chose Molly. If it had been anyone other than you, I might have been able to get over it. But since it was you, I just... don't think I can."

"Molly didn't choose Jackson over you," Grace told her. "She chose Grant, who has been working with your mom since last Christmas. He's the real reason Jackson is here—him spying on you was just a bonus."

Grace pulled a package of tissues out of her purse and handed them to Rebekah. "I didn't choose Molly over you either. I confronted her as soon as I found out who Jackson was and threatened to tell you myself if she didn't. I have been on your side this entire time, but you have to understand, I felt like I was between a rock and a hard place. The only option that didn't suck was to give Molly the chance to talk to you and explain her side of the story."

"So where is she then?"

Out of everything Grace had just told her, that was what she chose to focus on? Just once, could she catch a break? "She's back at her office."

"Of course she is," Rebekah sneered.

"Look, I'm not saying what she did was right, but this has been hard on her too."

Rebekah shrugged. "I suppose even Brutus had a moment of guilt when he stabbed Caesar."

Okay, fine. Desperate times called for desperate measures. Grace threw herself on the ground and wrapped her arms around Rebekah's legs, holding on for dear life.

"What are you doing, are you crazy?" she shrieked.

"I'm not letting go until you forgive me!" Grace said, refusing to let go even as Rebekah tried to break free.

"You're going to pull me down on top of you," Rebekah warned. She grabbed onto the nearest coffin, then shrieked again when it began to wobble. "Oh my gosh, you're going to kill us!"

Grace saw the wobbling coffin out of the corner of her eye but still refused to let go. "Then we die together! Which will make a lot of people sad, so you should consider forgiving me instead."

"Fine, I forgive you!"

"Really?" Grace looked up at Rebekah, her eyes narrowed in suspicion. "Or are you just saying that so I'll let go?"

"I mean it—now please let go before we both end up crushed!"

Are coffins really heavy enough to crush a person? She would have to look that up when she got home. They needed to be sturdy enough to hold a body but light enough for people to carry them. However, it did take many people to carry a coffin. Maybe it could crush them.

"Grace!"

"Oh, sorry," Grace said as she let go. She stood up and brushed herself off, thankful that part was over.

"You might be as crazy as Shelley!" Rebekah exclaimed.

Grace shrugged. "There are worse things in the world." She looped her arm through Rebekah's, then led her out of there and away from the offending coffin. "How about we go to Brynn's for some coffee? We need a treat after narrowly escaping death!"

"Fine, but you're paying. It's the least you can do."

"What's the most I can do?"

Rebekah thought about it. "Stop by the bakery and pick up a couple of those donuts to go with the coffee."

If she'd have known that's all it would take, she would have bought out the bakery on the way there. Oh well, nothing to do now but honor her friend's request. "Your wish is my command!"

Happy Mardi Gras!

Today was the official 'big day,' and Grace could not be more excited! If someone had told her five years ago—even one year ago—that she would get to host a Mayor's Masquerade Ball, she would have never believed it, yet look at her now!

But first, she needed to deliver on the promised scavenger hunt. She'd worked really hard on this, so she hoped her guests had fun... what few of them were left.

Jackson was currently M.I.A., Carl and Katherine had been going out to breakfast with Granny and Gladys for days now—and not returning till dinnertime—and Shelley was off who knows where, planning who knows what.

When the two couples walked into the dining room, Grace perked up. "Hey guys! Are you ready for your first clue?"

Jasmine and Eva exchanged looks, Jasmine's tinged with guilt.

"I'm sorry, Grace, but we're going to have to take a rain check," Jasmine replied. "Eva and I thought it would be fun to have a day of pampering before the ball, and the guys found this indoor golf club they want to go try."

It was difficult, but Grace managed to keep her smile intact despite her disappointment. "No worries! Have fun!"

She gathered up her scavenger hunt supplies and put them in a folder to be used for later. No sense in wasting a good event when she could use it for the next set of guests. But what should she do now? There were still several hours until it was time to get ready... which meant plenty of time to go check on preparations for the ball! So far, she hadn't had time to see the community center since the volunteers had decorated, and while she was out, she could also check on the ballroom.

Now that she had a plan, Grace was eager to get on the road, so she grabbed her coat and purse and headed outside, stopping abruptly on the porch when she saw the flurries falling gently to the ground. Her earlier excitement turned to concern as she worried about road conditions and the safety of her guests. Surely they wouldn't have to cancel the ball? She thought back to this time last year, when it snowed during her murder mystery event. Things had been fine then; she was sure they would be fine now.

The first stop she made was the hotel, but Jim's truck wasn't parked out front like it usually was. Did that mean he was done? She rushed inside and tried the doors, but they were still blocked. Maybe he forgot to unblock them once he was finished? She tried to call him, but he didn't answer, so she left a message and headed to the community center. Only, no one was there either. She tried the doors, but they were locked, so she decided to go to town hall and grab the keys. This was so weird. Where was everyone? The ball was literally hours away—shouldn't the community center be buzzing with activity?

Since it was freezing out, she drove the two blocks to town hall and parked right in front of the building, leaving her car running as she hurried inside. When she pulled on the door, it didn't budge. Okay, now she was worried. It was currently around ten on a Tuesday morning. Where was everyone? Why wasn't someone at town hall? Sure, Katie was gone, but wasn't Rebekah filling in for her?

Grace went back to her car and sat for a moment as she tried to figure out what to do. Normally, she would walk over to Molly's office and ask her, but after what happened yesterday, she wasn't entirely sure she wanted to go there. So, she did the only thing left she knew to do and called Rebekah.

"Hi Grace, what's up?"

"I'm calling to ask YOU that," Grace replied. "There's no one at the community center or town hall, and since we have a big event planned for tonight, I'm pretty worried about that."

"There's nothing to worry about. Everything is ready to go."

How was that possible? There were always last-minute things that came up, especially with events like this.

"Is there anything else?" Rebekah asked. *"I don't mean to rush you, but I'm at another event and I need to get back to work."*

"Of course, sorry," Grace said absentmindedly. She hung up the phone and decided to go to the farmhouse.

It had been a while since she had some time to herself—might as well enjoy it!

***

Grace turned this way and that as she checked her appearance in the mirror. Even she had to admit the green dress looked good on her. Was it fit for a queen? She carefully placed the crown on her head, then decided that yes, she did, in fact, look regal!

When she turned to the side again, she caught Cole's reflection and nearly jumped out of her skin! "You scared me half to death!" she gasped as she spun around to face him.

He grinned as he looked her up and down. "You must not have heard me come in," he drawled. "I must say, you are a sight for sore eyes." He moved toward her, his arms circling her waist as he pulled her into a slow dance.

"You're always a sight for sore eyes," Grace said as she leaned against him and allowed him to lead them around their bedroom. When the imaginary song ended, she reluctantly let go. "Guess it's time for you to get ready. Are you ready to be king for the night?"

"As long as you're my queen!" He kissed her cheek, then left for the bathroom.

While she waited, Grace went to the living room and looked through the sliding glass doors. Snow continued to fall and, from the looks of things, had been falling all afternoon. She stood there, mesmerized as the snowflakes twinkled like diamonds when they caught the moonlight.

Cole came up behind her, his familiar cowboy hat replaced with his crown. Her breath caught as she watched his reflection in the glass. Some days, she wondered how it was possible to be so lucky. Others—like today—she simply felt blessed he had come into her life.

"Are you ready?"

When she nodded, he took her hand and led her to the door, then grabbed her coat and helped her into it. She braced herself for the cold, then took one last look at her fur-babies, who were curled up and asleep in their beds. "Okay, let's go!"

Once they were settled in the truck, Cole handed her a blindfold. "Put this on, please."

"What's this?" she asked, taken aback by his odd request. "Am I going as Zorro?"

"Very funny," he replied. "Do you need help?"

Grace's brow furrowed as she looked between him and the blindfold. "No, what I need to know is why you want me to wear this."

"Because I asked nicely?"

It quickly became clear he had no intention of elaborating, so she had a choice to make. Did she trust her husband or not? Since he'd never given her a reason not to, she decided to go along with whatever this was, though for the life of her she couldn't come up with a single reason why he would ask this of her.

"If this messes up my hair, I'm going to be really mad at you," she said as she slipped the blindfold over her eyes.

"Don't forget, you called me the world's best husband the other day," he reminded her.

She snorted, then reached over and grabbed his hand. "Alright, cowboy, let's get this show on the road!"

"I believe the term you're looking for is 'your majesty,'" he teased.

"Stop making me laugh," she said, squeezing his hand. "My eyes are watering, and pretty soon I'm going to look more *Wednesday Addams* than *Mardi Gras Queen!*"

The truck began to move, Cole going silent as he concentrated on driving.

Grace tried to imagine the route in her head, listening for clues as to where they were going. Surely he was still taking her to the community center. But if so, why was the blindfold necessary? It's not like she didn't know they were going there.

Eventually, the truck came to a stop, the sound of nearby voices laughing and chatting announcing they had arrived.

"Can I take the blindfold off now?" she asked, her hand lifting to her face.

He reached over and grabbed her hand before she could, then brought it to his lips and kissed it. "Sorry, babe, not yet."

She let out a deep and dramatic sigh. "Fine. But you need to make this up to me later."

"Your wish is my command!"

His door opened, the cold blasting her from the side. "Wait there, I'll come around and get you."

Like she had a choice! Sure, she could open the door, but with her luck, she'd put her foot down wrong and end up breaking a heel!

Moments later, her door opened, another blast of cold hitting her from the other side. She felt his arms around her waist as he pulled her to him and out of the truck, then helped her stand. When she wobbled a bit, she grabbed onto the lapels of his coat to steady herself. This was ridiculous! And no way to treat a queen, mind you!

"Now can I take this thing off?"

"Soon, I promise," he told her.

He wrapped an arm tightly around her waist and began to lead her across what she assumed was a parking lot. Or perhaps a gravel road? Whatever it was, the surface was uneven and difficult to walk across in heels.

The farther they walked, the louder the voices became, and pretty soon, jazz music was added to the mix. She knew it! They were at the masquerade ball! But why the secrecy? She was starting to feel like a lamb being led to the slaughter, and it was not a good feeling.

To make matters worse, the music abruptly stopped, the voices ceased, and it became so quiet she could hear her own heartbeat.

"C-Cole?"

"You can take the blindfold off now," he told her.

She hesitated, no longer sure she wanted to know what was going on. But curiosity got the better of her, and she pulled it off, her eyes taking a moment to adjust to the light. When they finally did, she looked around in awe.

"SURPRISE!"

Grace looked up at Cole's grinning face, then back at all the masked attendees who were currently clapping as she took it all in. Somehow, Rebekah had managed to move the ball to the hotel after all, and the ballroom looked stunning!

The floors shone beneath her feet, the peeling wallpaper had been repaired. New drapes covered the windows, while the moth-eaten curtains had been removed from the stage area—the same stage that had obviously been repaired, as there was a band currently set up to perform. Then there were the decorations. A sea of purple, green, and yellow streamers mixed with balloons covered the ceiling. A wall of twinkling lights was draped behind the band, while tables lined the edge of the room with alternating purple, green, and yellow tablecloths, covered in beads and feathers. She had never seen such a festive room in her life. It even beat Christmas!

Rebekah waved to the band, who began to play again, then made her way over to Grace. "I can't believe I was able to pull this off," she said with a laugh. "You have no idea how many times you almost stumbled across my little surprise!"

"You did this for me?" Grace asked, her voice full of wonder. "Even though you were mad at me?"

"This took us all week to prepare," Rebekah explained. "And I was only mad at you for a hot second!"

"Wait a minute, how many people knew about this?"

Cole had the decency to look away, but Rebekah simply shrugged. "Pretty much everyone but you. Looks like you're not the only one good at keeping secrets, eh?"

Rebekah said as she playfully elbowed Grace. "Anyway, Mayor Allen will officially introduce the two of you as King and Queen as soon as we give people enough time to arrive. In the meantime, feel free to mingle as much or as little as you want."

Despite being a tiny bit miffed at him for keeping secrets from her, Grace accepted Cole's arm and followed him through the crowd to where her guests were seated. When they reached them, she did a quick headcount, relieved to see that everyone had made it, including Jackson. The one person she did not see was Shelley. Grace was still praying Shelley had other plans, but had no doubt her prayers were in vain.

"Hey everyone!" Grace called out, her voice raised over the music. "Are you having a good time?"

"It's great!" Jasmine said as she raised a glass of champagne. "I had no idea it would be so glamorous. I'm glad Eva and I got our hair and nails done!"

Eva nodded, a huge grin on her face. "I didn't think I would be, but I'm impressed! You sure know how to throw a party!"

Grace considered that high praise coming from Eva. "I had plenty of help!" she replied, unwilling to take all the credit.

Tap Tap Tap

They looked over to see Mayor Allen on stage, tapping on a microphone. "Good evening, everyone!" he said once he had their attention. "Welcome to our first-ever Masquerade Ball!"

The crowd clapped enthusiastically, many whistling and cheering.

"Let's get things started by introducing our very own King and Queen!"

More applause came as Cole and Grace made their way to the stage. They smiled and waved as the band played a little ditty behind them.

"CUT THE MUSIC!" Shelley yelled through a megaphone as she entered the ballroom.

She was gripping one of those selfie sticks with her broken hand—which had to be painful—and, of course, was wearing her signature wedding dress, in addition to a massive crown she had to keep pushing up on her head with the inside of her arm.

"Don't crown them yet!" she ordered. She turned to the phone and began to address her followers. "I'm here tonight to right the wrong that has been done to me. You see, *I* am the rightful Mardi Gras Queen! And that woman"—she pointed the phone at Grace—"stole my crown!" She turned the camera back to her. "Drop a crown emoji in the comments if you think *I* should be queen!"

Grace was grateful for her mask; she just wished it covered her entire face. For his part, Cole stood motionless next to her, his lips pursed as he watched the spectacle in front of him.

"Is it time yet?" a masked man asked from the side of the room.

"Oh yeah, I brought my own king," Shelley said with zero enthusiasm.

The man stood next to her, waved to the camera, then gave an exaggerated bow to the crowd.

"Stop trying to upstage me!" she yelled at him.

Ba Dum Tiss

Grace whipped around and glared at the drummer, but he couldn't see her through her mask. She motioned for him to cut it out, but he wasn't paying attention to her—he was watching Shelley, as if waiting for a cue. Was he in on her plans?

Shelley stared at her phone, then waved it triumphantly toward the stage. "See! Thousands of people are dropping crowns! I *am* the true queen!"

The band played the ditty again, Shelley eating up the attention as she preened for the camera.

At this point, Grace would happily give up her crown if it meant putting an end to this nightmare.

Mayor Allen tapped the microphone again. "That is enough," he said firmly. "Shelley, you lost fair and square. Either leave willingly, or we will be forced to remove you!"

"No can do, pops!" she replied. She set the megaphone down and handed the selfie stick to her partner, then ran over to a table and pulled out a confetti cannon. "Let's do this right! I, Shelley Erickson, am the one and only Mardi Gras Queen!" She fired the cannon, but instead of a large burst of confetti, a tiny ball popped out and landed on her partner's head.

The band played a celebratory song, while Grace hid behind Cole's back so the crowd couldn't see her laughing. Not that they were looking at her—they were too busy laughing themselves.

When the music stopped, the man ripped off the crown and threw it on the ground. "You told me this would WORK," he yelled at Shelley. "Look at this," he commanded as he showed her the phone. "They're asking if we got our crowns from BURGER KING!" He ran a hand down his face, pulling his mask off in the process. "Now they're calling me Rent-A-King!"

Grace gasped when the man revealed his identity. "Oh my gosh, that's Greg!"

"No, you don't understand!" Shelley protested. "This is a good thing! It's engagement! It means they love us!"

Mayor Allen tapped the microphone again. "May I have your attention!" He waited as the crowd turned back to him. "I would like to introduce your true King and Queen, Cole and Grace Reed!" He shook both their hands. "I am so sorry, but the only way to beat her is to ignore her," he told them. He signaled for the band to play, then left the stage.

"May I have this dance?" Cole asked Grace. He held out his hand, and when she placed hers in his, he led them off the stage and over to the dance floor.

The gang from the hotel joined them, and soon enough, the rest of the attendees did as well.

"Wait!" Shelley yelled. "I'm not done!" When everyone continued to ignore her, she stomped her foot. "This is all your fault, Greg!" She stormed out of the ballroom, Greg following close behind.

"I have a feeling people will talk about this event for generations," Cole drawled.

Grace sighed. "Yes, but not for the reasons I would have hoped."

Jake and Evie danced over to them. "I am so sorry!" Evie exclaimed. "There are no words…"

"It's not your fault," Grace replied. "I don't think there's a single person on this planet who could control that woman."

"You're probably right, but that doesn't make it any less embarrassing."

They danced away, leaving Cole and Grace alone again. As she swayed to the music, Grace looked around the room, her gaze wandering over all the happy couples. Some of them were expected, like Granny and Julian, and Rebekah and Thorne. Some took her by surprise, like Lyda and Jackson, and Jilly and Jim. But at the end of the day, the one thing that mattered was that they were together. And at the moment, there was no place she'd rather be!

G race stood on the porch wrapped in a blanket, coat, three layers of sweaters, two layers of pants, wool socks, and one of Cole's goofy trapper hats. More snow had come in overnight, and it was *FREEZING!*

But even though she offered to let her guests stay an extra day, they were determined to go home and get back to their lives. She was surprised to say she was going to miss this group.

While she always enjoyed hosting, she was typically ready for the guests to leave when the event was over, but this time she wished they could stay an extra day or two. She would have loved to take them up on those rain checks!

Jasmine and Dwayne were the first ones down, Jasmine as bubbly as ever.

"Okay, before I go, you *have* to tell me who that man with Shelley was last night! That was *the* craziest thing I have ever seen!"

"That was her ex-husband," Grace explained, though that was hardly an adequate explanation. "Or maybe he's still her husband?" Grace mused. "I'm not sure they ever officially divorced."

"They seem suited for each other," Jasmine said dryly.

That was the understatement of the century, but there simply wasn't enough time for Grace to give Jasmine a proper lesson in all things 'Greg and Shelley.'

So she smiled instead and reached out to hug the woman goodbye.

"Have a safe trip. You guys are welcome back anytime!"

"Thanks, Grace, we might just take you up on that!"

Grace gave Dwayne a quick hug, then waved as they walked to their car.

She'd gotten up early to shovel a path through the snow and was now glad she did, even if her arms and back disagreed.

Eva and Phillip came down next, Eva practically dragging Phillip along.

"Should I be concerned that you're in such a hurry to leave?" Grace joked.

"Not at all," Eva said as she gave Grace a quick hug. "We have plans to meet Jasmine and Dwayne for lunch, and I don't want to be late!"

The two couples' newfound friendship had been a happy surprise, and Grace was thrilled to see it continue once they left the B&B. Maybe she would see them all again someday.

"They just left, so you still have plenty of time," Grace assured her. "Have a safe trip. We'd love to have you back sometime!"

Eva waved as she dragged Phillip to the car.

"Bye, Grace," Phillip called over his shoulder. "Thanks for everything!"

She waved goodbye, then waited a few minutes to see if anyone else was coming down.

Carl and Katherine weren't leaving till the weekend and, last she checked, were currently resting after being out last night. Shelley had not been seen or heard from since she stormed out of the ball; in fact, Grace wasn't even sure she was there.

That left Jackson.

The door opened behind her, and when she turned to see who it was, Jackson appeared, sans luggage.

"Hey, Grace, can I talk to you for a minute?"

"Of course, what's up?" she asked. She pulled the blanket tighter while she considered moving this conversation inside.

Jackson shifted uncomfortably, his usual swagger replaced with nervous energy.

"I still have business I need to see to before I leave, and I was wondering if you would mind if I stayed for a while longer?"

He looked off to the side before turning his gaze back to her.

"I will pay, of course."

As long as she could still move back to the farmhouse, she had no problem letting him stay. And, hey, the extra money was always welcome!

"It's fine with me," she replied. "I assume Molly and Grant know about your plans?"

He nodded. "Rebekah does too. I think she said she planned to move back here today, so it will be nice to spend some time with my sister before I leave."

Hmm, that meant Grace would either have to evict Shelley or give Rebekah a different room. The first option held a lot of appeal.

"JOSIE!"

Grace and Jackson's eyes widened as they saw Gladys running over as fast as she could.

"JOSIE!!"

Granny rushed out onto the porch, a wild look in her eyes.

"What on earth is going on?" she asked as Gladys came to a halt on the porch. "I could hear you yelling over the TV!"

Gladys bent over and placed her hands on her knees as she struggled to catch her breath.

"They," she paused, breathing hard, "they chose us!" she continued to huff.

"Whose 'they,' and what did they choose us for?" Granny asked. She looked at Gladys like she'd grown a second head.

She stood up and screamed, "WE'RE GOING ON THE WHEEL!"

Then grabbed Granny's hands and shook them in excitement.

Shelley popped her head out the door.

"Did I just hear you say you're going to be on TV?"

"Let me be the first to congratulate you!" Jackson told Granny and Gladys. "I look forward to watching your episode!"

He excused himself, gave Grace an appreciative nod, then made his way to his car.

Grace waved, then turned her attention back to the others.

"Congratulations!" she said enthusiastically.

Her feelings were mixed, but she tried to be supportive since she knew how much this meant to them.

"Let's go inside so you can give us all the details," Grace suggested.

A syrupy sweet smile appeared on Shelley's face.

"Yes, come inside," she said, holding the door open wide. "We have lots to discuss, such as when *we* are going to California!"

Oh boy, Grace did *not* like the sound of that. However, it *would* get Shelley out of town...

She followed them inside, shutting the door behind her.

Just when she thought the fun was over, it seemed it was just getting started!

Afterword

Dear Reader,

Thank you so much for reading Countdown to Mardi Gras! I hope you had as much fun reading it as I did writing it! If you're curious as to what's going to happen next, Granny and Gladys are getting their own spin-off series! I just love those two characters and think it would be a blast to see them travel to California to be on Wheel on Fortune!

There will also be more Tess and Austin, and I think it's finally time to check back in on Valerie and see how she's doing down there in the Ozarks! If you haven't read Hope Blooms in Willow Glen, now is a great time to catch up! I am also toying with the idea of sending Bea, Maude, and Carol on a road trip together. I think the three of them together would be a hoot!

I would like to thank my good friend Angela Ratliff for giving me the idea to write about Mardi Gras, it was such a fun holiday to write about, and as someone who grew up in Louisiana, it made me a bit nostalgic! And thank you to everyone who voted for the Mardi Gras King and Queen.

It was so much fun to count the votes, and I loved having all of you involved!

I truly appreciate each and every one of you, and cannot thank you enough for your support. If you want to make sure you're always up to date on current news, you can join my newsletter at diannahouxshop/newsletter.

Happy Reading!
-Dianna

About the author

Hi! I'm a small-town girl who never outgrew her love for heartfelt stories and happily-ever-afters. I live in a rural Missouri town of twenty-five hundred people with my husband and three boys in a late 1800s home we're lovingly restoring—one project (and paintstroke) at a time.

When I'm not writing, I enjoy reading, perusing antique stores, or dreaming up my next story on the porch swing with glass of lemonade in hand!

My stories are seasoned with over-the-top, funny happenings in small-town settings, but at their heart, they're about real people with relatable struggles, hopes, and dreams. I write to entertain—and to remind readers that even the wildest moments can lead to something beautiful.